The Beast of Bear-tooth Mountain

BY
MICHAEL JOHN PETTY

THE BEAST OF BEAR-TOOTH MOUNTAIN
By Michael John Petty

Copyright © 2023 Michael John Petty
All rights reserved.

PAPERBACK ISBN: 9798862732078
PAPERBACK ASIN: B0CLG83RZ9
DIGITAL ASIN: B0CLCRSFVX

The Beast of Bear-tooth Mountain, or any portion thereof may not be reproduced without the express written permission of the publisher except for the use of brief quotations in a book review.

"Psalm 30:1-5" is a public domain hymn from the Lausanne Psalter.
For more information, visit PDHymns.com.

This is a work of fiction. Names, places, characters, and events are fictitious. Any similarities to actual events and persons, living or dead, are purely coincidental. Any trademarks, service marks, product names, or named features are assumed to be the property of their respective owners and are used only for reference and don't necessarily imply endorsement.

To request permissions, contact the publisher.

Cover design by Michael John Petty & Hannah Christine Petty

For Mom & Dad,
who always believed in me.

For Hannah,
who always encourages me.

For Lydia,
who I hope will never stop smiling at me.

The Beast of Bear-tooth Mountain

It was a cool morning in early May when Jordan and Deon hit the road, determined to finally ascend Bear-tooth Mountain. For years they'd been tickled by whispers of a breathtaking outlook from the top, which supposedly boasted the entire western side of the state. The summit's crisp air and unobscured views had piqued their interest then, and ever since they dreamed of conquering the craggily high place for themselves.

Though the lone mountain wasn't more than a few hours away from their remote college town, year after year, something always got in their way. A busted engine. A last-minute call to work. A family emergency. All these and more had kept them from the siren's call beckoning them to its crooked peak. But this time was different.

They knew that if they didn't climb it now, they never would.

Over the years, many had ventured to the top of Bear-tooth Mountain, though rarely did one attempt to trail it so early in the season. The locals knew that the snow near the top hadn't quite melted; that slippery sheets of ice still clung tightly to each rocky slab. Because of this, the Park Service usually advised against braving the trail until at least June. Even then, if the winter persisted, they might consider keeping the chilled tower closed until mid-July. However, even when the county failed to close the trailhead, it was said that the locals would often do so themselves.

But Jordan and Deon weren't deterred. Though perhaps they should've been. Having kept a close eye on the trail's condition in the week's prior, Jordan was confident that now was as good a time as any.

The two of them had spent considerable time hiking along the mountain range that divided their adoptive college home from its neighboring counties. Twenty miles was nothing to them, and though Jordan wouldn't be considered traditionally athletic (especially when standing beside Deon), he maintained a genuine love of the outdoors.

Spotting the three-fifty on the poor excuse for a road sign, Jordan pulled his Highlander into the dingy Gas-N-Sip just off the interstate. Unlike some of the nicer establishments closer to their artsy college town, this station looked a bit under the weather. Its rusty completion and greased-up underbelly weren't unfounded out here, but they didn't help much in attracting any new customers. Though perhaps that was the point.

Regardless, it would do the job, as it always had for the past fifty-plus years. As the nearest gas station for about

THE BEAST OF BEAR-TOOTH MOUNTAIN

sixty miles in either direction, it was the only option anyone ever had.

Before they came to a complete stop, Deon was already halfway out the door. He had struggled to remain in the confines of Jordan's Highlander, and after a few hours of sitting mostly still, he was jonesing for a release. "Last chance, you want anything?"

"I'm good," Jordan replied.

"You sure? I doubt there's another one as nice as this anywhere near the mountain," Deon said with a sly smile.

"Really, I'm good," Jordan replied, patting the backpack resting behind him. "I've got all the jerky I need right here."

"Suit yourself," Deon said with a shrug. He wasted no time, a handful of cash at the ready.

Jordan fed the pump some plastic before placing the nozzle into the fuel filler. His bare fingers were freezing, but that didn't stop him from gazing westward at the lone mountain ahead of him. As he turned back east, he caught glimpses of the warmth and light baking just beyond the horizon. Right on schedule. It wouldn't be long before they'd make it to the base of the mountain. From there, it would take most of the afternoon to hike up to the top. "Not a bad way to spend a day," Jordan thought.

As if on cue, his eyes shot down at his watch and caught the small hand leaping just past the seven. He watched carefully as the thinnest hand ran laps around the

MICHAEL JOHN PETTY

other two. Even if they'd been an hour ahead of schedule, it wouldn't have been enough for him. After all, he didn't wish to get caught all the way out here after dark.

The bell above the station's doorframe jingled an off-key clang as Deon barreled out towards the car, a thin "Thank You For Shopping" bag in hand. It had already begun to rip before he dropped it onto the car floor.

"Fair warning, the trail mix is mine," Deon said, passing Jordan a bottle of water. "No mooching after you get tired of your teriyaki."

Jordan ignited the engine and readjusted his back-facing mirror. "Just get in." His foot gently caressed the gas pedal, though he kept the Highlander in park.

"As you wish…" Deon said, ribbing on Jordan's favorite movie.

And so, their adventure continued. Within minutes, they were driving down an old country highway, passing through a handful of farming communities where the cows vastly outnumbered the people. It was a landscape they'd rarely explored, but one they thought was easy to fall in love with, if not just for the beautiful simplicity of it. It was so peaceful out here in the Middle-Of-Nowhere, U.S.A. Life seemed lived as intended. No unnecessary busyness. No pollution or smog. No year-long road construction. Just land and cattle and a big sky as far as the eye could see.

And then there was the mountain.

Neither of them had ever given this part of the coun-

THE BEAST OF BEAR-TOOTH MOUNTAIN

try any thought before. Sure, they had graduated from a school in a less-populated state, but their mid-sized college had most of the amenities that all the big cities had. But out here in the open wilderness, folks only entertained the essentials. Life was less wasteful that way.

Though they didn't quite understand it, nor would they ever choose this sort of life for themselves, they felt a deep longing for the old ways.

After about an hour, they passed through the small town of Carmel, if you could call it a town that is. It wasn't much, but it had the bare minimum. A local dive bar, a diner, a dual hardware-grocery store, and a post office littered Main Street. From there, they could make out the blanketed football field of the small K-12 school just a few streets over. But nobody was out and about today. *Nobody ever really was.*

For the spiritually inclined, there lay a lone Episcopal Church on the corner of Main and Stewart, and a local theater across the street if you were into the arts. Though by the looks of it, it hadn't been in operation for at least a few decades. It didn't take more than two minutes to drive from one end of Carmel to the other, and before they knew it, the undead town was long behind them.

"Not much out here, is there?" Deon watched as the

decrepit township retreated further into the morning's misty light.

"Not unless you're overly fond of cows," Jordan replied. "Or manure."

"Well, I'm not one to pass up a good burger, but this might be overdoing it." Deon pinched his nose and tried to forget how to use his fourth sense. Or was it the third? It didn't matter, within moments he was already palm-deep in the bag of trail mix he'd rescued from that worn-down gas station about 60-ish miles back.

"Dude, we're not even on the trail yet."

"So?" Deon shrugged. "*I've* got plenty of snacks. You're the one who only packed jerky."

Jordan rolled his eyes. "It's not like we're hiking Everest."

"Hey, I gotta keep up my strength, you know?"

Jordan noticed a positive change in the speed limit and stepped on the gas. He took a long look at the shadows creeping across the open range as the sun climbed higher. If he'd known his breath would fail him, he might've scheduled an earlier starting time; but as it was, he kept on track, trying his best to take it all in.

"Would you ever wanna live in a place like this?" Deon asked. He too had been studying the painted landscape.

Jordan glanced out the car window. His eyes glazed over the wheat fields, still littered with snow. They passed farms with broken-down pick-up trucks and rusted trac-

THE BEAST OF BEAR-TOOTH MOUNTAIN

tors loitering beside storage sheds and barns. Yes, there was something pure and good about this simple way of life. Though, simple didn't mean easy. Frankly, Jordan wasn't sure he'd make the cut.

"I just don't know what I'd do out here," he said. "It's not really my scene."

Minutes passed before they stopped alongside the narrow country road, just near the trailhead. On the curb across from them sat a ramshackle Dutch Reformed Church that somehow looked even older than the rest of the quaint little town. Watching them with fading stained-glass eyes, the church sat just opposite the trail's gaping mouth, carefully guarding the mountain.

But, like most, they paid the chapel no mind and began mindlessly collecting their gear and provisions. They had been sure to fill their packs the night before to not waste time this morning. A few liters of water, emergency supplies, a gas stove, and a half dozen heating packs in case their fingers got too stiff. They had everything they might need for this journey. There was more, of course, Jordan was a "worst-case scenario" sort of guy, always prepared for things to go wrong.

Or so he thought.

Though he understood Jordan's pessimistic view, Deon opted to live life a bit more optimistically. Maybe it was the way he was raised, but he chose to hold to a confident expectation of good. Nevertheless, he strapped his father's

7

old hunting knife to his belt, just in case.

After donning their burdens, they were ready to embark. Jordan looked up at the mountain and then back down at the windy trail. The trail itself was lined with trees on either side, with some of the branches overlapping above to form a sort of makeshift covering. The scent of the pines wafted towards them like an oven filled with freshly baked bread, pleading with them to begin. Though wildfires had raged in previous summers, these welcoming lands looked relatively untouched.

A smile crept across Jordan's face. It was just as he had imagined it. After all these years, after all the talk, they were finally here. He glanced back down at his watch and noted that it was the top of the hour. They had timed everything perfectly; or rather, *he* had. He turned back to Deon, who crouched down finishing the laces on his boots.

"You ready?"

Deon tightened his double knot and jumped to his feet. "As I'll ever be. Can you believe we're really doing this?"

Jordan locked the Highlander and turned towards the trail. It was time.

As they took their first steps in the soft, sweaty snow, they heard a creaky voice beckoning them from behind. It started out just above a whisper but soon became louder, and frantic. "Good morning, lads!"

Jordan and Deon glanced back at the older gentleman

THE BEAST OF BEAR-TOOTH MOUNTAIN

waddling his way towards them from the churchyard across the street. He was a short feller, of average build who clad himself a black overcoat and a felt hat. He wore big, round glasses and though he looked as if he should've had a great, white beard, he maintained only a few unkempt gray whiskers peppered across his face.

From what they could tell, he was the only one out here at this time of day. And no wonder as there wasn't much out here to begin with. More than likely, they were the first visitors he'd had in a week, if not longer.

"Just our luck," Jordan muttered. He resisted the urge to glance back at his watch. *This better not take long*, he thought to himself. When the man in black reached them, he offered an open palm. He seemed friendly enough, so they gave theirs back in return.

"I am very good with faces, and I do not recognize yours," he said, a warm smile plastered across his face. "Reverend Jude Anthony, at your service."

Jordan wasn't exactly thrilled. He wasn't expecting company, nor did he much care for it. He wouldn't be deterred again, not when they were so close.

Noting Jordan's frustration, Deon went on defense. "Good morning, Reverend. I'm Deon, and this here is Jordan."

Deon knew how to play the field. After four years of college ball—and the complimentary years as Jordan's roommate—it had become second nature. Jordan sent back a courtesy wave, but his eyes itched toward the dark tower behind them.

"Nice to meet you both," the Reverend said. "Where are you gentlemen headed this fine morning?"

"Isn't it obvious?" Deon replied. "We're headed up the mountain. We've been trying to get out here for quite some time, but..."

"Something always got in the way," Jordan snapped back.

Either unconcerned or ignorant, the Reverend seemed oblivious to Jordan's irritable tone. "Now, why on God's green earth would you want to climb *that* mountain at *this* time of year? It is far too dangerous. Much slipperier than you might think! You ought to reconsider."

Had the minister left it there, the boys might've just considered him a harmless old man with nothing better to do than worry about the health and safety of complete strangers, not unlike the little, old ladies who police nearby playgrounds where children climb as high as they can on the tallest trees. But the Reverend didn't leave it there.

Instead, he rambled on, explaining that it was crucial they let the snow melt completely before returning to ascend the high place. It wasn't long before he trailed off, listing all the local predators that the boys were already keenly aware of. Even Deon was beginning to lose his patience now.

"You would be better off heading back home," the

THE BEAST OF BEAR-TOOTH MOUNTAIN

Reverend finally said. "Or, better yet, come on inside, out of the cold. We could share a pot of warm tea and you can tell me all about your dreams and ambitions."

"Thanks, but we can handle the cold," Jordan said, with more than an ounce of pride curling from his lips. "Enjoy your tea."

With that, the boys turned away from the old man. First Jordan and then, somewhat apologetically, Deon followed suit as they started back down the trail. Deon wasn't too pleased about abruptly turning their backs on a minister (he'd been brought up better than that), though he couldn't help but be glad to leave the old man behind. The last thing either of them wanted was another reason not to see their course through to the end.

They didn't get too far before a faint chill perforated their ears and sunk down to their uneasy stomachs. "You must not go!" the minister cried, standing like a crazed watchman at the city gate. His feet were firmly planted in the snow. He showed no intention of moving even a step closer toward them, or the mountain.

Jordan couldn't help himself. He glanced back at the pastor with a fiery look in his eye that was about to cut loose. He somehow managed to hold his peace, but it took every last drop of patience he'd packed with him. With a heavy sigh, they turned back to the minister, though they kept their distance.

"Believe me or do not, it is entirely your choice, but

11

I would caution you against journeying up *this* particular mountain at *this* particular time of year. There is a beast that resides in its heart. A beast that only exhumes itself when the mountain dethaws, to hunt and gather for its expected slumber."

"A beast?" Deon asked, "You mean like a bear?"

"Nice try. Bears only hibernate in the winter," Jordan said.

"This is no bear," the minister continued, letting his words linger a moment more. "This creature is something else entirely. It is a carnivorous beast capable only of death and destruction." His eyes widened as he spoke. "If you ascend Bear-tooth Mountain now, you may never return."

Jordan couldn't help but laugh. Any pent-up rage he'd been holding dissipated as he erupted like a middle-school science class volcano. He couldn't stop himself. A man-eating monster inside the mountain? Please. If it were true, someone would have surely said or done something about it by now. Someone with a little more, scratch that, *a lot more* credibility than this raving small-town preacher. If the Park Service didn't know about any monster on Bear-tooth Mountain, then what secret knowledge could this kook possibly offer? Even Deon was stifling his laughter now, trying to help Jordan regain his composure.

"This guy's a lunatic," Jordan whispered.

"He's probably just lonely," Deon whispered back. "Let's just let him be."

THE BEAST OF BEAR-TOOTH MOUNTAIN

Jordan caught some loose tears amidst his laughter. "No disrespect, Reverend," he fibbed. "But this isn't our first mountain. We can handle ourselves just fine. And if we see any strange beasts heading our way, we'll just run like hell."

"I really think you boys ought to come inside," Reverend Jude pressed. "Your very lives may depend on it."

"No thanks," Jordan said. He glanced down at his watch, signaling Deon to help wrap things up.

"We appreciate the warning, but we're prepared for any predators," Deon said. "Anyway, we've better get going if we want to stay on schedule."

Reverend Jude considered his next words carefully. For a moment, neither Jordan nor Deon thought he'd speak at all. But he did, and he did so with a hint of grace upon his lips.

"Very well, then. I wish you boys a safe and uneventful journey. I will pray for a speedy return."

"Thanks," Deon said. "We appreciate that." *He really did too.*

"Just mind the caves," the minister warned as he wandered back to the old church across the street. His muttering continued the farther he waddled. "Mind the caves…"

After the Reverend pulled the chapel doors closed, Jordan and Deon finally set sail. They pushed the minister's eerie warnings aside and began their trek into the snow-covered forestlands that led to the base of the mountain.

Their journey had officially begun.

As they marched upward, Jordan and Deon were overcome by the winter wonderland around them. The snow glistened in the sunlight, flickering like stars in the night sky. Even though the winter was melting away, it was as breathtaking as they could've imagined. Had it been closer to Christmas, Deon might've hummed some carols, but as it was, they hiked the first leg in silence. Some untouched snow lay carefully on the trees, attempting to conceal the mountain's peak as they trudged forward. Their only complaint was the half-melted slush that covered the actual trail itself, which marred their footing. Hoping to avoid any aimless wanderings upon their return, Jordan was careful to leave clear orange markers along the path.

The only tracks they could make out in the slush were those of deer and squirrels, but there was little doubt that other creatures were watching them from afar. So long as they weren't predators, they welcomed any spectators to their uninteresting sport. Jordan even thought he saw a white rabbit brush past them, but it had either been a trick of the eyes, or it had escaped under Mother Nature's frosty blanket.

But despite the beauty around them, Jordan couldn't shake the crazy preacher's words. His wild eyes, his strange manner of speaking. It was all a bit ominous and unsettling,

THE BEAST OF BEAR-TOOTH MOUNTAIN

which was the last thing he wanted this day of all days.

"What makes people like that?" Jordan finally asked. It came out as a question, but he didn't really expect an answer.

"Like what?" Deon said.

"Crazy."

"You talking about the Reverend?"

"Who else?" Jordan replied. "Hard to think he's anything but when he spews on about flesh-eating monsters living inside the mountain."

"I think we could've been a little kinder to him," Deon admitted. "I'm sure he has no one else to talk to."

"Gee, I wonder why."

"Jordan…"

"And the way he kept trying to get us to come inside. Like he was going to try and convert us into some weird cult or something," Jordan continued. "I don't trust that guy."

"You don't trust most people."

That was true, Jordan did have a hard time trusting others, but that didn't mean he was wrong about the Reverend. "If there was something actually up here, someone would've found out about it by now," he said.

"You're probably right," Deon replied. "But we still could've been a bit kinder."

It took only two hours for Jordan to finish his last bits of jerky. As predicted, hunger had welled up inside him

MICHAEL JOHN PETTY

and it soon occurred to him that he hadn't eaten much since they began their road trip early that morning. It wasn't intentional, he'd been so preoccupied preparing for the actual event that, as usual, he'd forgotten the most important meal of the day. Maybe he ought to have bought something at that last oasis, after all.

Still, he'd rather let his stomach rumble until lunch than admit that something so basic had slipped his mind, especially after so carefully preparing everything else. So, he toughed it out by taking large gulps from his water bottle every few minutes.

Of course, Deon saw right through Jordan's bravado–he'd known his friend long enough to recognize when he didn't want to admit to a mistake–and offered Jordan a handful of trail mix to stop his gut from stirring.

"We should probably stop for lunch pretty soon," Deon said. "But that'll hold you over until then."

Jordan scarfed the snack down without so much as a breath. He was a little more than embarrassed, but he quickly buried those feelings and sheepishly thanked Deon while dropping another orange marker in the snow.

"Don't mention it," Deon said.

They lingered on a moment more before Deon stopped. He turned to Jordan with an easy grin plastered across his face.

"Well, actually," Deon began. "That girl that lives across the hall from you," he said. "The cute one with the

THE BEAST OF BEAR-TOOTH MOUNTAIN

golden doodle…"

Jordan instantly regretted his life choices. He knew *exactly* who Deon meant. He'd been failing to muster up the courage to ask her out for weeks.

"Chloe?" he finally muttered.

"That's right, Chloe. I was wondering if you could do something for me?"

Jordan caught his sigh; he knew where this was going. It made sense. She probably wouldn't have been interested in him anyway. Jordan was a bit on the lankier side and not particularly outgoing. Certainly not the specimen that Deon was. The only reason they were even friends was because they'd been randomly assigned as roommates their freshman year. Despite Jordan's antisocial tendencies, Deon made every possible effort. He was the outgoing one. One of those people who always tries to get to know every single person around him. Jordan, on the other hand, was just the weirdo who tagged along.

"Yeah, sure," Jordan finally answered. *It's not like they were dating anyway.*

"Great!" Deon said. "I want *you* to ask her out."

Jordan was stunned. He stood still with his mouth agape. His thoughts spun faster than propellers on a helicopter. He was barely sure which way was north. It took a second before he could fully process Deon's request. "What?"

"You heard me. You should ask her out."

Jordan didn't know whether to thank his friend or to hit him. He wasn't ready for that yet. She hardly even knew he existed. He had no shot with a girl like that. More than likely, he'd be friend-zoned by the end of the week. He *almost* wished Deon had been interested after all.

"I'm not blind, you know," Deon said. "She might not know you're into her, but you can't hide that from me."

"I don't know," Jordan said, stumbling over his words. He was breathless, and his palms were getting sweaty. "I don't think she'd be interested."

"Why not? You're smart. Outdoorsy. Sometimes you're funny."

Jordan mock laughed. He wasn't looking for a pep talk or a pity party. More than anything, he wanted to stop talking about his lack of a love life altogether.

"Jordan," Deon said as he stopped them dead in their tracks. "What have you got to lose? You ask her, she says *no*, no big deal. You have your answer. But if she says *yes*…"

That's what Jordan was afraid of.

Around eleven, the boys stopped for lunch. After igniting their portable stove and cooking shared cans of beans and potatoes, they ate. It wasn't the tastiest meal they'd ever devoured, but after a morning of hiking through the cold, it hit the spot. Especially for Jordan.

The snow was quite soft beneath their feet, though

THE BEAST OF BEAR-TOOTH MOUNTAIN

patches of deceptively smooth ice hid silently beneath. Both Jordan and Deon fell more than once, but they wouldn't let themselves be defeated by any minor inconveniences or dashed pride. The scenic trail and warm meal were more than enough to keep them going. That and the pine-tinted air that regularly refreshed their lungs.

Their short break wouldn't last, however, and they'd be off again in no time. As they continued upwards, they noticed an eerie stillness that crept upon them like a mountain lion silently stalking its prey from the trees. They no longer heard any birds overhead or trucks on the distant freeway. The crunching of snow beneath their feet was the only sound caught consistently by their ears save for their breathy exhales between footsteps.

To pass the time, they reminisced on their not-so-long-gone college days. Deon brought up the time Jordan passed out at the local hot springs, having shifted too quickly from the springs to the freezing river. The rushing water had sent a shock to his system that blurred his vision white and made his ears ring for the better part of an hour. He was terrified then, and though all their other "friends" had left him behind, Deon stuck around.

Deon *always* stuck around.

The pair had made lots of fond memories together over the years, some good and others not so good. When Deon's father died their sophomore year, Jordan accompanied him back home to offer additional support and condolences.

To say it had been awkward for Jordan would be an understatement. He didn't know anybody, nor did he have any profound words of wisdom, but it had been the right thing to do. Jordan didn't know it, but his being there helped Deon not feel so alone. Likewise, when Jordan's mother battled cancer, Deon helped raise the necessary funds to pay for her treatment. The costs had been absorbent, and without Deon's vigorous fundraising efforts, they might not have succeeded. But, after nearly a year of chemo, she was in remission and doing well.

If anything could be said about these two, it's that they were brothers, through and through. Which made Deon's news all the harder to share.

"I have something I've been needing to tell you for a while," Deon stuttered.

"Okay," Jordan said. He wasn't one to beat around the bush and preferred that others do the same. "Just say it."

"I was offered a position at a tech startup. It's a lot of the same stuff I do now, just for more money and better benefits. It's kind of a once-in-a-lifetime opportunity."

"That's great!" Jordan said, correctly anticipating the other shoe to drop.

"Yeah, it is," Deon stumbled. His gaze was fixed downward. "The only thing is, it's in Salt Lake City."

"Oh," Jordan replied. *What else was there to say?*

"They want me out there by the end of next month, which I know is around your birthday but…"

THE BEAST OF BEAR-TOOTH MOUNTAIN

"You should take it." Jordan wasn't sure why he said it. He wasn't even sure he meant it. But he said it anyway.

"Yeah?"

"Yeah. Sounds like a sweet gig."

"Salt Lake's pretty great too," Deon added. "And don't worry, I won't be converted or anything."

That made Jordan chuckle, but he quickly shut back down again. His mind was swimming. No. Drowning. How could he just up and leave? And so soon. In the absence of any answers, Jordan checked his watch. At least their upward trek was still on schedule.

The next few miles were a bit quieter. Deon made a few more excited comments about Salt Lake and the possibilities that this new position might offer, though Jordan didn't say much, save a few vague questions about the job. Deon tried to soften the blow, reminding him that they'd still be under eight hours (or a quick flight) away. But it didn't make it any easier. Before long they weren't speaking at all, and the sound of their boots kissing snow reigned supreme once again.

Jordan checked his watch again just after one. The peak was nearly in sight; they were on the home stretch now. The air was thinner up here, and crisper too. An uneasy wind bit at their chapped lips as they huffed through deeper mounds of snow toward the top. Their packs had

MICHAEL JOHN PETTY

gotten heavy, and their legs were slowly turning to rubber. Up here, a deep, long breath was almost as refreshing as a cool drink of water, though a bit harder to come by.

The snow-capped forest had disappeared and been replaced by earthy formations and icy boulders, towering over them on either side. From up here, Jordan and Deon could see the sleepy town of Carmel clearly below, in all its disheveled glory. They could barely make out the roof of Jordan's Highlander from behind the tree line, though the old Reformed church stood clear as a watchtower opposite the trailhead.

That didn't exactly make Jordan feel any better.

He was still convinced that the crazed preacher might slash their tires to trap them there before ritually sacrificing them later. But he couldn't think about that now. He had too much on his mind after Deon's bombshell. Of course, he tried to drown those thoughts too, plodding on solemnly through the snow.

The mountain was so heavily forested that, at times, they had hardly been able to make out the sky above them. Here though, they basked under that great heat lamp in the sky and took a minute to shed their winter gear. They'd worked up a mean sweat. It was only a matter of time now before they reached the top, and even Jordan could admit the need for reprieve. Though that didn't stop him from anxiously watching the time.

As they took a seat on the nearest rock, they found

THE BEAST OF BEAR-TOOTH MOUNTAIN

themselves lost in the serenity. All seemed well.

And then Deon heard a strange rustling in the distance.

"What was that?" he said, shaken from his peaceful meditation. He couldn't quite make out what he had heard.

"What?" Jordan replied. He didn't hear anything.

"Shhh…" Deon heard it again. *Was it a growl? Maybe a shriek?* "That! Did you hear that?"

"Hear what?"

Deon put a careful hand to his ear. "Listen."

Jordan took a moment to focus on the sound. He heard nothing but the swaying of trees and the occasional whisp of the icy breeze gliding past him. He was beginning to wonder if his friend hadn't watched one too many scary movies. But then again, Deon didn't like scary movies.

"I'm not crazy, I heard something," Deon insisted. "Close your eyes." He was serious about this.

Jordan humored his friend but remained unconvinced that Deon was hearing anything other than a small critter darting through the trees. Sure, it could've been a predator, but that seemed unlikely too. But after a few moments, Jordan heard something himself, something he couldn't quite put his finger on. It was gruff, and fierce. It didn't sound like any animal he'd ever heard.

"What is that?"

"I don't know," Deon whispered. They sat there for a moment, carefully deciphering the strange disruption coming from the trees. "Do you want to find out?"

Deon already knew Jordan's answer. He didn't even have to look to know that Jordan's cadence had dropped. Or that he was already checking his watch. They were on a tight schedule, and even a few extra minutes threatened to throw it off entirely. Deon knew that. He didn't want to hike back down in the dark either, but his curiosity was getting the better of him.

This wasn't uncommon. Deon always liked to have a story primed for whenever he was thrown a lateral in casual conversation. It kept him current, and interesting. Whenever they were out with their peers, co-workers, or even complete strangers, Deon was always known for being the guy with the crazy story, even if that story wasn't his own. If this sound turned out to be something, like a bear stumbling out of its slumber or even a group of teenagers fooling around with matches (thought that seemed unlikely), it would be a month's worth of material at least.

As Deon predicted, Jordan glanced at the tiny hands on his wrist and calculated their next steps. They were already half an hour behind schedule, though he'd neglected to mention it. He wasn't in the mood for another adventure, especially concerning something so inconsequential to their primary objective. If this was to be their last big "hurrah," then Jordan didn't want any unscheduled surprises keeping them from summiting the top.

On the other hand, with Deon leaving so soon, their time together was glissading quickly through the hourglass.

THE BEAST OF BEAR-TOOTH MOUNTAIN

They might not have many of these adventures left. With that in mind, Jordan chose to indulge his friend's curiosity. And, if he was being completely honest, he was curious now too.

Following the strange sound, Jordan and Deon headed back down the mountain. Jordan wasn't overly enthused about this sporadic side-quest, especially since it meant backsliding on their original campaign, but he could tell that Deon enjoyed the spontaneity. They so rarely did anything together that would be considered spontaneous (usually Jordan had planned their itinerary down to the letter), so this all felt a bit *unnatural*.

Whenever they binged a handful of action flicks, Jordan scheduled everything from the snack selection to the best time to take a bathroom break in advance. If they were going downtown for drinks, he accounted for the distance between bars and the varying atmospheres and clientele of the different establishments. This "go with the flow" mentality didn't flow naturally for him, but for the sake of their friendship, he was willing to comply. At least for a while.

What are we doing? Jordan wondered, wishing they'd remained on the designated path. The nearer they got to the cluster of trees just off the trail, the clearer the sound became. It didn't sound like an animal, at least not one from around here, though it had a rough complexion to it. *Almost machine-like.*

That was their impression from afar anyway. The gravelly cadence made Jordan uneasy. His hand crept down to the bear spray hanging off his belt and he soon found his fingers wrapping carefully around the freezing canister. Deon did the same.

As they continued, they paused every few yards to catch a better whiff of the sound. Sometimes they heard it, but other times an eerie silence took over. But after nearly twenty minutes, they were ready to call it quits. They could barely hear it anymore, and Deon could tell that Jordan had lost all interest. His irritation was as clear as a bad tattoo.

"Sorry I wasted our time," Deon said with a sigh. He took a seat under a large pine, a look of defeat plastered across his face. "I thought it might be fun, you know?"

Jordan didn't.

"Oh, forget it." Deon's mood had turned sour too.

"It's not a waste," Jordan replied, fighting the urge to check the time. "Who knows what it was." He didn't know what else to say after that.

The two of them sat in silence for a good while as they considered their next move. A delicate breeze danced around them like a lost butterfly, but they paid it no mind. They knew they needed to finish their quest soon if they wanted to make it down the mountain before dark.

Despite that, neither one of them knew how to re-

THE BEAST OF BEAR-TOOTH MOUNTAIN

sume their journey. Within minutes, a heaviness had crept over them like a thick mist on an open road. Not even the brights on an eighteen-wheeler could get through it. They hardly wanted to do anything at all except sit there in silence. It was as if a spirit of dread had blanketed them, keeping them from pressing forward. Worse than any road-block they'd encountered before, they almost didn't care to see the top of Bear-tooth Mountain at all.

This was unlike anything they'd ever experienced. They had dreamed about this trip, about seeing the immaculate view from the top, for what seemed like forever. The thought of coming all the way out here, only to stop so close to the top, seemed on one hand like insanity. On the other, it felt good and comfortable. Right, even.

Jordan had nearly dazed off when a long moaning sound bellowed from beyond the tees. It echoed across the blanketed wilderness like a foghorn, sending invisible spiders crawling down their spines and lasting much longer than they'd hoped. *Was it a call? A cry?* Whatever it was, they could hardly bear it and it shook them from their sudden slumber.

"What was that?" Jordan asked. He had jumped to his feet but could hardly stand.

"I don't know," Deon said, "but I don't think we should stick around to find out." He slowly unsheathed his father's knife.

But before they could move, they felt the ground rumble beneath them. The snow shifted, and the trees gave up some of their excess. *An earthquake?* Jordan wondered, but it didn't feel like any earthquake he'd ever experienced. He hadn't been in many, but he knew this wasn't one. This quaking had a sort of beat to it. A rhythm.

One... Two... Three... Four...
One... Two... Three... Four...
One... Two... Three... Four...

Again and again, it continued. Louder with each new thud. They were speechless. Worse than that, they could hardly even think. They were petrified with fear. *Could it be an avalanche?* There didn't seem to be any snow headed their way. In any event, they couldn't be bothered to care. They simply stood peering helplessly into the darkened forest.

The rumbling continued. The same consistent pattern but getting stronger and stronger. Each quake was more intense than the last. The trees began to sway as if an otherworldly force had snuck upon them.

"Let's go," Jordan finally said, almost in a whisper. Deon didn't argue.

As men possessed, they shuffled out and away from the clearing, bolting as fast as their packs would let them before realizing that they had no idea where they should go. They scanned the clearing for somewhere to hide, but their options were scarce. A mound of snow. A gang of rocks. At this point, they'd take a hole in the ground. But there was nothing. No real cover as far as their eyes could see.

It was then that Jordan spotted a dark crevice in the brush behind them nearest the mountain's stony hide. He almost hadn't seen it, thinking it was nothing more than a shadow at first, a trick of the light. But he could see now that this shadow was their only chance, and he wasted no time running to it.

"Follow me!" he shouted.

As Jordan peered into the sudden darkness, his head was fully consumed by the black. Without warning, his arms and legs quickly followed, and soon there was nothing left of him at all. In an instant, he was gone.

"Jordan!"

Deon watched helplessly as Jordan vanished into the mountainside, as if by magic. He didn't believe in magic, but he didn't have time to tell the mountain that. Beneath him, the shaking grew more intense, and if he wanted to escape whatever was causing their panic, he had no more time to spare.

"God, help me," were the last words Deon uttered before impulsively diving into the black himself.

The darkness was thick and penetrating. It had passed over them upon entering the mountain's hidden chamber like a thick smoke around a campfire. Jordan and Deon had traded in one danger for another and now, surrounded by shadow, they were about to discover the hidden secrets of Bear-tooth Mountain.

They could still feel the ground drum beneath their feet, accompanied by a muffled groan that sounded not unlike someone on the opposite side of a car door. They couldn't make out any distinct words, but that didn't ease their fears one bit.

Jordan fumbled through his bag with a frantic urgency. They couldn't see a thing in here, and though he had no reason to pack one, this was the exact scenario that made Jordan glad he had brought a flashlight. Ignoring his newfound blindness, Jordan found his electric torch within seconds, flipped the switch, and fired a pure burst of white light directly into Deon's eyes.

"Watch it!" Deon snapped.

"Sorry," Jordan said, redirecting his beam. He was careful not to shine it too close to the entrance, opting instead to light up the deep end of the cavern. While they weren't sure what was outside, they also didn't know what might be lurking in the darkness with them.

"How'd you find this place?" Deon asked.

"I don't know," Jordan answered. "I just saw the crevice, I guess. The next thing I knew, I was inside. I called you, didn't you hear me?"

"No," Deon said. "But thank God for this place. A little stuffy for my taste, but it's better than nothing."

"What was that out there?" Jordan said.

THE BEAST OF BEAR-TOOTH MOUNTAIN

"I was about to ask you the same thing."

They reveled in the silence for a moment. Neither one of them knew what it was, nor did they have any realistic theories. They briefly entertained the thought that it could be an animal of some sort, but the strange noises coupled with the quick tremors didn't give them much hope.

"Maybe someone else is up here," Deon said. "Other than us."

"Yeah, maybe…" Jordan said, unfocused. It irked him that nothing was adding up. "I bet it's that preacher," he finally said. "Something wasn't right about him."

"He literally told us to stay *off* the mountain," Deon replied. "Why would he do that if he didn't want to keep us from running into something up here?"

"Didn't you ever watch Saturday morning cartoons as a kid?" Jordan said. "The bad guy *always* tries to throw off suspicion by pretending to buy into some hokey urban legend that they're secretly using to concoct some sort of real estate scheme." Jordan was trying to convince himself as much as he was Deon.

"Real estate, huh?" Deon didn't buy it. Neither did Jordan if he were being honest, but he was grasping at any straw he could find.

Deon swapped the flashlight from Jordan's fingers and squeezed past him. He guided the light towards the rocky path in front of them, deeper into the cave. "Woah," was all he could say as he studied the dark tunnel.

The pathway seemed to stretch for half a mile, though it actually ran quite a bit further. The tight cavern walls rounded upwards and had either of them been any taller, they would've been forced to crouch. As they stood, they had a little wiggle room above their heads, though they'd have to walk single file to advance in either direction.

As Deon examined the back, Jordan turned to look at the front. He hadn't noticed before, but the cavern's entrance seemed to be covered by a thin shadow, presumably from the brush that guarded it. But the longer he looked, the more distinct the covering became so that he realized that it was no shadow at all. Now looking closer, it appeared to be a dark film that kept the crevice hidden from anyone—*or anything*–that might be wandering the mountain.

Speaking of the mountain, Jordan was again itching to resume their regularly scheduled program, hoping to salvage the rest of the daylight they had left. He glanced back down at his watch before he heard Deon gasp, the light now pointed at the mouth of the cave.

"What on earth?" Deon said.

Jordan's eyes followed and saw the same strangeness that Deon's did. In step with the floor's drumming, an enormous shadow glided past the entrance. This wasn't the strange shadowy film that Jordan had just discovered, but something on the outside trying to look in.

"Turn it off," Jordan whispered. He lurched for the flashlight and quickly powered it down. They stood care-

THE BEAST OF BEAR-TOOTH MOUNTAIN

fully in the darkness as they watched this shadow pass, making the blackened cavern all the darker.

The mysterious figure moved back and forth around the entrance for what seemed like an eternity. Soft vibrations surged through the ground, and they could hear a gust of breathy wind followed by the violent snapping of branches. A low growl murmured its way among the brush, rounding out the high strangeness before them. Whatever it was, it seemed like it caught their scent.

Despite its closeness, whatever lurked outside was either unable to penetrate the cave or unable to find it. *Or maybe it's toying with us*, Jordan thought. Each time it growled, the hairs on the backs of the boy's necks stood in salute. Deon carefully placed his back to the cavern wall, breathing as intermittently as possible. The beast, whatever it was, sounded much too large to be a bear and made more noise than a bobcat or a mountain lion ever would. Somehow, they knew that whatever it was, it wasn't going anywhere any time soon.

Of all the things that Jordan had planned for today, this was not on his list of potential happenings. A bear encounter, sure, that was possible. The cave was plausible too. He even half-expected an avalanche at this point. But this? This was something else entirely.

While Jordan thought on his itinerary, Deon was slowly turning white. His lips moved quietly with no discernable words spoken. For as carefree as he often seemed to be, Deon could only hope that the Good Lord would hear his silent plea in the dark reaches of this place.

As Deon communed with the unseen, he gripped Jordan's shoulder, squeezing it something fierce. It hurt, a lot, but Jordan refused to move any more than an inch. Not until he was sure that whatever was out there was gone.

After what felt like an eternity (but was really just under an hour), the beast, whatever it was, had left. At least, as far as Jordan and Deon could tell. The drumming beneath their feet had faded into nothing, and the rustling among the brush had finally ceased. They were alone, and there was real comfort in that. The boys hardly whispered throughout their entire close encounter, and the tight cavern walls had made them a bit claustrophobic.

They breathed easy now.

"Okay, we're okay," Jordan finally said, letting out a long-awaited breath. He needed to stretch his legs but resisted the urge to leap out of the cavern. Just because that thing wasn't waiting at the door didn't mean it wasn't right around the corner.

The pair slid down the craggy walls opposite the other, the pressure finally off their screaming soles. Jordan hydrated himself and Deon followed suit after first unbuttoning his jacket and wiping the half-dried sweat off his brow. They didn't much care that they were nearly out of fuel,

THE BEAST OF BEAR-TOOTH MOUNTAIN

they were just thankful for the reprieve.

"What the hell?" Jordan said, taking in another quick huff of dusty air.

"You're asking me?" Deon replied, his voice trembling. "All I know is that was no bear."

"What then? A moose?"

"Not like any I've ever seen. Or heard."

"Then what?"

Deon took another gulp of water and shook his head, a disapproving frown formed across his lips.

"I don't know, and I don't wanna know. All I know is that that was no bear, moose, lion, or animal I've ever heard." Deon drew in a few more uneasy breaths. This was a story alright, but he'd have to make it home first before telling it. "Had to be a bigfoot or something, man. I don't know what else could make that kinda noise. And that shaking? That thing was like a tank."

"Elephants can make the ground vibrate," Jordan offered, trying to explain it any way he could. They knew beforehand that the mountain had its fair share of predators, just like any other trail or preserve in the state, he just never thought they'd actually encounter one. "It's so rare up here that they don't even have a sign," Jordan remarked a week prior. Turns out, he'd been gravely mistaken.

"Jordan, come on. We're not in Africa, or India, or anywhere near a zoo." Deon fiddled with his hunting knife, flicking it every few seconds.

"What should we do?" Jordan asked. He was good at putting a solid hiking schedule together, but he was no strategist. More than that, he wasn't much of a leader. But Deon knew how to play the field, and Jordan was counting on that.

"Well, we shouldn't go back out there until we're a hundred percent sure it's not just waiting for us."

That much was obvious. They didn't want to walk right into its jaws, claws, or whatever sharpened features that thing might be brandishing.

"Maybe another hour?" Deon said. "Then we can head back down."

Jordan nodded in agreement. That made sense. If it had been left up to him, he might've suggested that they make a mad dash down the mountain, so he was glad that Deon axed that right off the bat. Jordan wasn't an idiot, but he was scared, and fear makes people do stupid things. He checked his watch. The sun wouldn't set for another few hours, so they'd still have most of the daylight. Not that this thing seemed to care much about the cover of darkness.

"Although, there could be something hiding out in here," Deon added. He wanted to make sure that they covered all their defenses.

"I didn't think about that," Jordan murmured. He turned the flashlight back on again and directed the beam toward the darker end of the tunnel. As far as they could

THE BEAST OF BEAR-TOOTH MOUNTAIN

see, there was nothing lurking in any shadow or crevice. Though, how deep the cavern flowed was still uncertain.

"We should keep an eye on both ends," Deon said as he gripped his knife.

Jordan agreed and the two of them shuffled into position, back-to-back. An uneasy blade shivered in Deon's hand as he faced the mouth, while a can of unused bear spray and a wobbly flashlight rested in Jordan's as he stared into the dark end. Each hoped the other would offer to trade sides, but neither of them dared move.

The minutes on Jordan's watch passed as they sat in undisturbed concentration, like gargoyles warding off any unexpected evils. Despite not making it to the top of the mountain, they were both happy to be alive. As they each watched their respective charges, they could hear only the soft echoes of their breath along the slick cavern walls.

"So," Deon said, breaking the silence, "You still mad at me?"

"For making us chase that thing or for leaving?"

Deon chuckled. "Both, I guess."

"I'm not mad," Jordan muttered, telling only a half-truth. "It's good, right? The job's a good thing?"

"Yeah, I think it is."

"Then I'm happy for you."

Jordan let that hang for a moment. It wasn't entirely a lie; he really was trying to be happy for his friend. Opportunities like this don't come every day, and Deon was right, Salt Lake really wasn't *that far* away.

"When do you leave?"

"Not for a few weeks," Deon said.

"Plenty of time for more adventures then," Jordan said, forcing a broken smile. He bounced the light sporadically across the walls and into the black as Deon nodded, relieved. He'd hoped that the news wouldn't strain things between them. He'd hoped that this would be something of a fresh start, a new chapter rather than an ending. Sure, that wouldn't be without its own set of challenges, but they were challenges that they'd face together.

"You better come visit me," Deon said jokingly. It wasn't really a joke, but he was still hoping it would come across as one.

"Of course," Jordan said, distracted. As they'd been talking, his attention became divided by the innards of the cave. He shone his light along the bruised walls as if he were looking for something. He'd been so focused earlier on the weirdness of the cave mouth that he never got a decent look at this end. As long as they were stuck in here, he might as well take a look around. Anything to pass the slowly ticking time.

"What are you doing?" Deon nudged.

"Wait a second," Jordan said. "I think I found something."

Jordan got up and followed his light stream just a few feet from his station. He was careful to keep an eye on

THE BEAST OF BEAR-TOOTH MOUNTAIN

the black hole beside him and occasionally flicked his light into the tunnel to be sure they were still alone. He placed a steady hand on the rocky wall, careful not to touch the object of his focus.

"Hey!" Deon said, refusing to move from his post. "Are you just gonna leave me here in the dark?"

"Hold on," Jordan muttered as he pressed forward. He glanced at what appeared to be detailed markings on the wall. Scratch that, they were *drawings* of some sort. Paintings. Native American by the looks of them, though he couldn't quite discern the tribe. One thing he could make out is that they were old. Very old.

"Come take a look at this," Jordan said as he waved Deon over.

"No," Deon said. "Someone needs to keep an eye out."

"Just come over here for a minute."

Without much more of a fight, Deon joined him, though his eyes routinely flashed back to the entrance of the cave. He wasn't about to let his guard down.

Jordan had all but forgotten his post by now and was focused intently on this newfound gallery. It helped keep his mind off the danger. More than that, the academic in him had taken over like a fox in a hen house. Maybe this side-quest wasn't such a waste after all.

"Looks like Native drawings of some kind," Deon acknowledged. He went to touch one of the painted figures before Jordan grabbed his hand.

39

MICHAEL JOHN PETTY

"They're *pictographs*," he said. "And they're in perfect condition."

Deon took the hint as Jordan redirected his flashlight. In a moment, he found the painting's wellspring and eased them toward it. Soon they would have more questions than answers.

"It starts over here," he said.

The boys took stock of the image. At first, they weren't sure what to make of it, other than it being a collection of scribbles that formed some sort of pattern. But the longer they stared, the clearer the picture became. It was as if by looking at it with intention they were able to somehow see something that wasn't there before. The images came into focus. A new story had begun. *Or was it an old story made new?*

At the top of the first pictograph sat a design that looked to be either a star or some majestic-looking heavenly body. Unlike the usual depictions of these celestial fireflies, what made this star stand out was the face embedded in the center. It was an ominous face, with dark, square eyes that gazed upon them. Piercing as headlights on a dim highway. The mouth wasn't much better; the ends crept up into a slight curl that felt more sinister than amused. Jordan noted that it wasn't so different from the faces on those sun and crescent moon designs that litter local gas stations and pawn shops. But that wasn't the most interesting part.

Below the roguish star sat what appeared to be six men.

THE BEAST OF BEAR-TOOTH MOUNTAIN

Well, it looked more like they were kneeling than sitting, though they did so with their spears in hand. These curvy caricatures were oriented in an upwardly submissive angle towards the sky-ward creature, almost like they were…

"They're worshipping it," Deon whispered, "Like a god."

They moved on to the next image, this one more bizarre than the first. Here, the star-being had additional human features. Adding to its beaming face, it had grown a newfound torso and legs that shot straight down. The now incarnated creature's arms were spread wide, as to gather more tribesmen to himself. Beside the star-man stood the men who had first worshipped the heavenly being. Their tribal headdresses gave them away, though this time they weren't alone. Alongside them, were what seemed to be women and children. Jordan noted that the men no longer bore their spears, trading in their weapons for idle hands that gestured toward their female counterparts.

"So, what? He demands worship from the entire tribe?" Deon asked.

"Something like that. But it's just a legend," Jordan dismissed. "Nothing short of a myth or fairy tale."

"Not like any fairy tales I've ever read," Deon said.

"You haven't read the originals then."

The next pictograph was the most gruesome yet. The star-man stood in the center of six of the women who had been with them prior. They were dressed in white gowns

41

with braided hair, though, unlike the previous image, they weren't standing in awe of their new god, they were…

"Dead," Deon quivered. The word seemed to echo right off the walls. "They're all dead."

As the tribeswomen lay dead on the ground, their blood trailed upwards toward the mysterious sky-creature. The men, once their protectors, were nowhere to be found. No, these women had been offered up willingly, but that wasn't all. As if the sacrificial massacre wasn't enough, the star-man held six circled faces above his head, each bearing the same sinister grin that the tribal deity wore, though their hair better resembled that of the women who lay dead on the floor.

Deon shivered. This was all becoming too real for him. He knew he shouldn't be afraid, but something inside of him was tugging at his innards, screaming for him to listen. "I don't like this, man."

Jordan wasn't surprised at Deon's reaction; ghost stories weren't really his thing. He preferred a good action-comedy and the occasional fantasy epic to any spooky horror flick. But Jordan prided himself on embracing most genres, though, even he could admit that this was a bit too horrific.

"It's just a story," Jordan said. As he took a deeper look, he noticed a correlation between the women's deaths and the new faces, but he couldn't quite put his finger on what exactly that connection was.

After checking both ends of the cave for peace of mind

THE BEAST OF BEAR-TOOTH MOUNTAIN

(they were still safe), they continued on to the next image.

As they gazed back at the wall, all color melted from their faces. In this snapshot, there were six giant men, larger than buffalos, who towered over the normal-sized tribesmen. These giants wore the same grimmed eyes as before, though their expressions had changed. Instead of sly, suspicious smiles, these giants looked warlike, wrathful. Their lips curled like lions' jaws as they pounced on their prey below. The tribesmen, who had reclaimed their weapons, were fighting these monsters off as the rest of the women and children high-tailed it in the opposite direction.

One of the giants held a full-grown man in its six-fingered paws, a blood-tipped spear lying still on the ground. Unlike the others, this captive was missing his head. Blood smeared across the giant's face as if it had bitten into this man like a piece of chocolate, savoring the crunchy flavor. It was a truly terrible sight, one that would stick in their minds for a long time. But even this wasn't the end.

"Dear God" were the only words Deon could get out.

"These things were people-eaters," Jordan whispered. "Giant six-fingered cannibals."

"They don't look too human to me," Deon noted. "What kind of sick story is this?"

They looked back on the previous image and counted the small faces above the star-man's head. Six. The same number of giants in the last pictograph. These things had been born, no, bred through some sort of ritualistic means

43

MICHAEL JOHN PETTY

for the sole purpose of ruling these lands as their own. At least, that's how it looked according to legend.

The next few images detailed a tribal uprising of sorts. Those who survived the giant purge wandered to meet with other tribes, who in turn unified into even greater numbers. These groups banded together to lead a revolt against the shaggy-headed beasts, beheading them as their own people had once been beheaded. The story chronicled a triumph after all.

"Well, at least there's a happy ending, I guess," Deon said, wishing Jordan had never found these drawings in the first place.

"That's interesting," Jordan muttered.

"What is?" Deon was being kind; he didn't really want to know.

Jordan pointed at the dead giants painted on the wall, decapitated by the mountain's natives. "I only count five."

"Huh," Deon said, taking a closer look himself. "Maybe it's a mistake?"

They looked back at the previous pictographs and re-counted six creatures birthed from the star-man's magic. Likewise, there had been six full-sized giants who terrorized the people. The numbers just didn't add up.

"Not likely at mistake," Jordan pondered out loud. "These people were careful to paint the same amount before… Something must've happened."

They kept on, ravenous for the story's end. On the next

THE BEAST OF BEAR-TOOTH MOUNTAIN

set, they saw other star-beings arrive to carry their wicked counterpart away. By the looks of it, they had wrapped the bent star-man in some sort of bond that it was powerless to stop, burying it deep beneath the earth. But what was most interesting about this image was not the civil conflict amongst the living stars but what lay in the background. As soon as they saw it, they recognized the jagged edge that sat proudly at the top of a larger mountainous base.

"Is that what I think it is?" Jordan asked.

"It has to be," Deon replied. "It hasn't changed a bit in all this time."

Behind the star-beings stood what looked to be Bear-tooth Mountain itself. Its signature peak glared at them like a haunted house atop a haunted hill in the most haunted town you could imagine. Of course, there was no town there yet, not in the painting anyway, but the idea was fixed in their minds.

The next image nearly overtook them. It was certainly not for the weak of heart, and it pounced on them so quickly that they thought they were under attack. Fear swelled within their stomachs and their bones felt cold.

A frightening and distorted face, one that mirrored the giants from before, screamed back at them. It was the last pictograph on the wall and by far the most unsettling. Jordan flashed the light downstream to confirm, but it was true. They were left alone with this horrible face and it's deep, dark eyes that seemed to follow them as they moved

MICHAEL JOHN PETTY

back and forth along the wall. Its gaping mouth covered everything else, and they could almost hear a growl bellowing from behind its jaws. Beside the face sat a red handprint. The paint must've been especially wet though, as small streams trickled down to the cavern floor. By the looks of it, it had been painted a long time ago.

"I don't think that's paint," Deon said, thinking to himself that if he ever heard another ghost story again, it would be far too soon.

"What is it then?" Jordan mocked. "Blood?"

"None of the other paintings dripped down like that," Deon replied. "And none of the others were that... Red."

"Like I said, fairy tales. This is all just an ancient superstition. A story these people told to explain their lost history, nothing more. None of this is real!"

"I don't know, Jordan. After what we saw today..."

"What did we *see*?" Jordan snapped back. "A shadow moved across a cave wall. Big deal. It could've been anything."

"The ground shook beneath us. We heard a sound like nothing we've ever heard," Deon began, he was practically shaking now. This legend, as Jordan deemed it, had made an uneasy home for itself beneath his skin.

"You sound just like that crazy preacher," Jordan sneered.

"Yeah, well, maybe he's onto something," Deon said, wishing now that they had heeded the old man's warnings.

46

THE BEAST OF BEAR-TOOTH MOUNTAIN

"We should've never come up here."

"What? We've been talking about this for years, man! And now you just want to throw it all away? Because of some crazy cave paintings? No wonder Salt Lake was an easy choice."

"There's truth to everything, Jordan," Deon said, hiding his hurt. "Maybe even something like this."

Jordan snarled. He couldn't believe that Deon, of all people, was falling for this. They'd both taken the same Native American studies classes in college; heck, Jordan even graduated with a minor. But to take these old legends, which were passed down orally across generations before being depicted here, as historical fact? He'd always respected Deon's religious upbringing, but this was pushing it.

"Tell you what," Jordan said. "I'll prove to you in under five minutes that there isn't a giant monster out there or in here."

Jordan plopped down his bag and pulled out a small box. Unloading the contents, he put together an even smaller box, this one sporting propellers on each end. It was a drone and a nice one at that. Had they made it to the top of the mountain, Jordan had planned on capturing a complete ariel view of the surrounding landscape. But given the circumstances, now seemed like the right time to boot it up.

"We're gonna send this thing outside first to see if anything's out there," Jordan began as he flipped on the drone's headlights. "Then we'll send it down the tunnel, and when you see that there's nothing down there—"

"That's a terrible idea," Deon interrupted. "We already know something's out there. We want it to go away, not wait around."

"Fine," Jordan said, "then we'll send it down there first." He pointed at the pitch-black abyss behind him. "And when there's no demon hiding in the dark, except for maybe a sleeping mountain lion, we'll know that all this is nothing more than folklore." He clicked a few more buttons before connecting the portable flying machine to his even smaller cellphone. "After that, I'll send it into the forest, and you'll see that there's no giant monster waiting for us out there either."

"If there is something down there, we shouldn't mess with it," Deon said, his final protest.

Jordan rolled his eyes, though Deon couldn't tell in the dark. Having successfully set up his drone, he sent the robotic scavenger into the void in search of answers. Jordan was confident that they'd find some, and anyway, this would help pass the time and take their minds off that strange Native American horror story as they waited out whatever had been stalking the cave entrance.

They watched carefully on his phone's display as Jordan weaved the mechanical moth down corridors and past stalagmites, none carrying the slightest hint of intelligent life. No crack or crevice was left unexplored, and though they

THE BEAST OF BEAR-TOOTH MOUNTAIN

expected to find either a surprise cougar or a grizzly, they didn't even spot a loose hair.

The innards of the cave were beautiful, even on the small, night-vision green display. The walls sparkled as the drone's light touched the sweaty fragments, glistening off the formations like a disco ball. Eventually, the cave opened into a grotto. The ceiling extended much higher than they'd imagined, like a two-hundred-year-old cathedral towering over a small European town. A calm, thin stream ran through the middle of the room, zigzagging across the floor. They weren't sure where the water was flowing from, but they were amazed at the winding stream as it passed without a care through the darkness.

"Wow," they said, almost in unison.

They couldn't help but take it all in. Had Deon not been so frightened, he would have wanted to explore further, but as it was, he was happy to be viewing the mountain's interior from the comfort of a screen. He pointed to a darker corner on the edge of the grotto, past the stream and hiding behind a looming shadow. "What's over there?"

"Who's curious now?" Jordan smiled.

He piloted the airborne scout closer to the dark spot to get a better view. It was hard to make out at first. Piles of rocks were gathered, each more ragged than the last. The light helped a little, but Jordan realized that he was too close to make anything out. He pulled the drone back a smidge to get a better look and immediately they wished he hadn't.

To their horror, they realized that these weren't stones at all; they were bones.

They had no words; they could only stare in awe at the makeshift mountain comprised of littered human remains. It seemed impossible. *Someone must've found this cave before they did, right? How could this many people have died here?* They must've been Native American, probably hundreds of years old. Maybe the mountain was some sort of burial ground, and this was their last warning.

Before they could notice, the "low battery" icon flashed in the corner of Jordan's phone screen. Desperate for their attention, it blinked rapidly before finally giving up altogether. Without so much as a beep the phone died, and the boys sat helplessly in the dark.

Jordan and Deon didn't know what to do. They had no way of knowing if that thing was still out there, and now they'd lost the best chance they had at finding out. If they journeyed further in, they'd be going in blind. Whatever tore apart those dried bones in the first place might come after them too. If they attempted an escape down the mountain, they wouldn't make it very far if that beast were still lingering about. It was a no-win scenario, except for maybe whatever that thing was out there.

"I'll be right back. Then we can figure all this out,"

THE BEAST OF BEAR-TOOTH MOUNTAIN

Jordan said. He was already preparing himself for the trip.

"Are you crazy?" Deon replied. "We still have no idea what's down there."

"Shhh," Jordan whispered, putting a lone finger to his lips. "Keep it down."

"Exactly. We can't go down there, Jordan. It's not safe."

"And we're safe now?"

Jordan had a point. It wasn't a comforting point, but it was an obvious one.

Now Deon was contemplating a mad dash down the mountain. Maybe he could outrun whatever was out there? If Jordan stayed in the cavern, away from the opening, he could probably make it down within the hour, call for help, and bring the authorities back with him. It wasn't much of a plan, but it sounded a whole lot better than dawdling around in the dark. Especially knowing that something else had been in here first.

"For all we know, those bones are hundreds of years old," Jordan said, pulling Deon away from his foolish plan.

"I don't think we should risk it," Deon replied.

"Fine," Jordan said as he began packing up his things. "You stay here and watch the entrance. I'll be right back."

"You're not going down there alone."

"That drone wasn't cheap, Deon. I'm not leaving without it."

Suddenly and without warning, Deon grabbed Jordan's arm. It stopped Jordan dead in his tracks. This was

51

the most forceful Deon had ever been with him, and he once had to stop Jordan from wandering off a cliff while his nose was deep in a map. Jordan stopped then just as he stopped here, as if shaken out of a hypnotic daze. Except this time, he didn't thank Deon for saving his life. This time, his shock turned to anger.

"Let go."

"I'm not going to let you get yourself killed over a stupid robot."

"It's not a robot, it's a drone, and it cost half my rent," Jordan said. "I'm not leaving it here to rot when we already know nothing's in there."

"But whatever's out there probably knows that we're in here," Deon replied. "It may be too big to squeeze its way in here, but out there in the open, it would have home-field advantage."

Jordan sighed at the sports metaphor. He clenched his fist a little, but soon let it fall. He dropped his backpack and leaned against the craggy wall in defeat.

"Whatever," Jordan sighed. "You win."

Deon let go and slumped to the ground relieved. He was exhausted. They both were. This trip hadn't quite been what they'd expected. With tensions so high, Deon was thankful that things hadn't erupted. He took a load off and closed his eyes, his head fixed on a dent in the wall.

But before he could take another breath, Jordan snatched his flashlight and bolted down the dingy corridor.

THE BEAST OF BEAR-TOOTH MOUNTAIN

Faster than Deon could turn his head, Jordan was off, disappearing now for the second time into the black.

"I'll be right back," Jordan whispered as his light slowly faded away.

Deon couldn't see a thing, hearing only the echoes of waning footsteps on the cavern floor. He couldn't believe his luck.

Jordan ambled down the cavern with a tight grip on his flashlight. He could tell the batteries were beginning to fade even though he'd replaced them the night before. He hadn't figured on using them for hours on end, or that they'd be anywhere particularly dark at all. Their hike was meant to be a day trip, they were supposed to be back by sundown. He once again commended himself for bringing the light in the first place but then flinched at the thought of extra batteries. *Nobody's perfect*, he reassured himself.

As he retraced his lookout's steps, he pondered the origins of the human remains they'd discovered. *It was probably just a group of travelers who'd gotten lost*, he hypothesized. *Or maybe that preacher had something to do with it...* Either way, he didn't think much about it again after that. He cared only about finding his drone and getting out of there. He checked his watch, though mostly out of habit. He didn't even register the time. Not that it mattered now, he'd given up any hope of a timely exit and would instead settle for a safe one. Though he didn't believe there were any predators lurking in the dark, he couldn't escape the sinking feeling that he was being watched closely. But he soon rationalized that too.

As he crept down the long cavern, Jordan arrived at the open grotto. As his light bounced around the wide-spread room, it was clear to him that there had been nothing to worry about. Awestruck, he gazed at the glistening stalagmite formations as he shone his light upon them. The images his fallen soldier had reported back didn't do them justice. He could better hear the lapping of the trickling stream now and he bent down to scoop up a long sip. It was heavenly, like drinking from a spring that might've granted him eternal youth or happiness. He felt blessed to have stepped foot in such a hidden paradise, and though the lack of sunlight (among other things) left a lot to be desired, he wished that Deon was there to experience it with him.

Having been easily distracted, Jordan promptly remembered why he was there. He crossed the stream and soon found himself quickening his pace. He flew to the other side of the hidden chamber and in only a moment stood before the pile of bones.

It was a thorough collection of remains, with all two-hundred and six variants represented in some misshapen or crushed form. By the looks of it, there were dozens of bodies here, though it was impossible for him to tell how

THE BEAST OF BEAR-TOOTH MOUNTAIN

many or how old they might've been.

Jordan looked at the empty sockets as they stared back at him with hollow tidings of toil and trouble. Instantly, he saw something grim in the fleshless faces that he'd recognized before. Something he saw in the face of the old preacher who lived at the base of the mountain. Fear fell upon him like a wet blanket in winter, and he felt powerless to escape it. It had crept up his spine and petrified him. It was impossible to move. His limbs nothing more than phantoms.

Jordan could barely tilt his head downward to lay eyes on his powerless lookout. It took all his strength to lower himself to the ground. His neck was fixed so as to not trade glances with the creeping shadows around him.

He never felt more alone.

There. His frozen fingers wrapped around the drone. Easing himself back up, Jordan took a deep breath. "It's okay, I'm okay," he said, slowly turning around.

And that's when he saw it.

A dark, humanoid figure of above-average build stood there. It taunted him with its stillness, studying him. Jordan was terrified, and it took everything in him not to scream or lose consciousness. His flashlight quaked in his hand and had he not been suffocating it in his grip, he may have accidentally reunited his drone with the dusty floor. Instead, his stiffness turned to sickness as his heart pounded on his chest, hoping to break through.

"Did you get it?"

Jordan didn't know whether to shriek or to expire, so he did the only thing he could think to do. He flashed the light directly at the figure and was beyond relieved when he saw that it was Deon. His ever-faithful friend had followed him even further into the mountain after all. He didn't deserve him, and he knew it.

"It's you!" Jordan said, nearly shouting.

"Who else would it be?" Deon said. "Keep your voice down."

"I-I thought you weren't coming..."

"Well, I couldn't let you die in here."

Before they could take another step, the bones behind Jordan began to rattle. The ground beneath them offered a batch of familiar tremors, continuing in the normal four-piece intervals. Dirt and dust rained from the ceiling, and even the stream in the middle of the grotto seemed to shake. Whatever it was, it felt exactly like what they'd experienced before.

"We have to get out of here," Jordan said. Deon didn't disagree.

The pair shot their way back through the open hall and quickly picked up their pace. The rumbling got stronger, and the ground proved increasingly unreliable. In all the commotion, Jordan tripped and bashed his leg against a sharpened edge. The cut ran deep across his upper thigh and stung like nobody's business. Jordan cried out in a

THE BEAST OF BEAR-TOOTH MOUNTAIN

burst of pain, trying to scramble back to his feet.

Without missing a beat, Deon doubled back for his friend and lifted him off the cold, hard floor. But Jordan didn't care about his leg. His sole focus was on his prize. "The drone! Where is it?"

Within seconds, Deon found Jordan's fallen soldier. It was completely shattered on the rugged ground beneath them. The propellers were bent or broken. The camera busted. Even the body was scuffed beyond repair. "Crap. Sorry, man."

But Jordan didn't have time to mourn. The rumblings felt like an earthquake now. It was harder to move by the minute. It was as if whatever was causing the quaking had picked up speed and was moving at full force. Before long, Deon's prior suspicions were confirmed as a guttural growl rang throughout the mountain's deep and hollow halls.

"Come on, we're almost out!" Deon yelled as he helped Jordan along.

Finally, they crossed the depleted stream and laid their eyes on the cavern entrance: the small one-person corridor that led back to their initial hiding place. It wasn't perfect, but they both understood that whatever was out there was either unwilling or unable to pursue them further once inside. It was their only hope of survival.

Jordan was barely hanging on but moving as fast as he was able. Sweat poured from his face as he held his gashed leg with one hand, his other firmly around Deon's shoulder.

MICHAEL JOHN PETTY

Truthfully, Deon was carrying them both now, but what else was new? As they hobbled towards their salvation, the quaking suddenly stopped. An eerie silence fell over the room. Only the sound of Jordan's panting comforted them.

"Do you hear that?" Deon said.

"Oh no, not this again," Jordan replied, fighting the sharp burn in his lungs.

The noise was faint but familiar. In a normal setting, full of crowds of people and flickering fluorescent lights, Deon wouldn't have thought twice about it. It was a sound he was used to hearing and one he'd grown accustomed to from the discomfort of his helmet while playing college ball. But here, in this god-forsaken earthen chamber, it was the most unsettling thing he could ever have hoped to hear.

"Breathing," he finally said. "Something's breathing."

Deon slowly turned to peer into the mountainous cove. It was pitch black, so he shifted his flashlight slowly across the room. The light reflected off the sweaty moisture on the stalagmites and shimmered in the stream that ran through the center. He could even make out the bones in the back corner and the remains of Jordan's drone not far off. As his light moved further left, towards the massive opening on the other end of the grotto, he finally caught a glimpse of it.

It was big, nearly as tall as the room itself, with massive legs the size of small tree trunks and hairy arms just as thick. It bore a wild, reddish mane that flowed about its

THE BEAST OF BEAR-TOOTH MOUNTAIN

head and down the better part of its chest. Its eyes nearly reflected the light when it hit them, just like those of a black cat in a dark alleyway. Though it wore no clothes, its natural covering spread across its large, sculpted body. It snarled a deep snarl, which grew from the recesses of its throat. Almost as if it were licking its lips, it opened its gaping mouth to reveal double rows of teeth that looked more like two legions of newly crafted arrowheads.

Without giving them another moment's peace, the creature charged them as a sharpened war cry escaped its bloodied, chapped lips. Deon pushed Jordan forward as they made the final sprint back towards the tunnel. Jordan had barely seen the thing himself, and though he couldn't quite make out its full appearance, he could tell by Deon's urgency that they were in grave danger. His leg throbbed like a hundred bee stings, but he refused to give it a second thought. He gave this last push his all, running as if his life depended on it.

This time, it did.

He had been moving so fast that he hadn't realized that Deon was no longer holding him up. He was running just as well on his own. His breathing was the heaviest it had ever been, and he couldn't remember a time he'd been forced to run like this before. As he darted through the tunnel, he realized that the only way to be sure of their escape was to also bolt down the mountain. Not wasting any more time, and knowing that Deon was following closely,

59

he blew right past the pictographs, right past his backpack, and right on out of Bear-tooth Mountain.

Once outside in the cold, fresh air, Jordan stopped. Breathless. He knew that whatever that thing was couldn't reach them through the tunnel. Given the time between their first escape and this one, he figured they'd be safe for a few moments before they scurried away from this profane space. It wasn't until he had sufficiently inhaled that Jordan realized an even uglier truth, one that he couldn't easily ignore or forget.

Deon wasn't behind him anymore.

Jordan couldn't breathe. His thoughts ran aimlessly, with every mental image transfixed on the tunnel. On that snarling sound they'd heard. On that bent creature they saw. Having been consumed by his throbbing leg, he hadn't seen but a glimpse of the beast, though he noted its abnormally large figure and the soft glow of its eyes against the light. For as big as the giant was, it moved faster than he'd imagined, blurring toward them like a gust of wind before a thunderstorm.

Deon is dead, Jordan thought, rationalizing his retreat. *He couldn't have made it out in time.*

He thought about peeking back into the cave, at least as far as where he'd left his pack. Maybe he'd find him there under the pictographs, in shock and gasping for air. Maybe

THE BEAST OF BEAR-TOOTH MOUNTAIN

he was just out of the creature's reach, and then they'd be back to where they started.

If that was true, then Jordan was running out of time. It would undoubtedly resume its hunt soon, which would only lead it back outside. Back in the open. He needed cover, and he needed it fast.

His eyes scouted the frosted wilderness. There were no signs of life save for a few birds far off. Even from a distance, they were a comfort, but not enough to ease his scattered mind. Deon would be safe if he stayed within the tight cavern, and if Jordan could make it down the mountain, he could bring back help. It was obvious that most folks around here didn't know about the creature that lived within the Bear-tooth's earthen walls. Or at least they didn't talk about it. It must not venture very far from the caves.

Jordan pondered his next move. If he could hobble fast enough, he might make it down the mountain before dark. He glared at the descending sun and opted to check his watch instead. It would be tight, but he could do it.

He had no other options.

Before Jordan could take another step, he heard a shout from among the darkened trees. It was short, and a long silence held afterward. Within moments, he heard the pitter-patter of feet glopping through the melting snow. The footsteps were consistent, one after the other like a single water droplet leaking from a broken faucet.

But Jordan wasn't taking any chances. He took cover,

guarding himself with a thick, prickly brush.

It didn't seem to be the creature, the ground would've shaken, but he couldn't tell what else might be out there. Fear trickled down his mind like venom, stiffening every aching muscle and stilling his spine to a halt. Though it probably kept him alive, he was beginning to loathe his anxious tick.

"Hello? Boys?"

The voice was familiar. It was a man. The call rang through the trees once more, clearer now. It was an *old* man.

Jordan could see the figure clearly now as he continued towards his position. A bloodhound came into view, following the hobbling man through the slushy snow. A quick bark escaped the canine's jaws before the old man tried again.

"Is anyone out there? I mean you no harm."

It was the preacher.

Jordan forced himself quiet, which was hard given that he was still shaking. He didn't know if he could trust this man. Part of him was elated to see the minister out here searching for them. The Reverend's story of a strange beast now made a lot more sense, and, in hindsight, he appreciated the unheeded warning. On the other hand, he knew nothing about this small-town preacher, or his connection to this thing, and that didn't make him feel any better.

"Jordan! Deon! Oh, please let them be alright…"

THE BEAST OF BEAR-TOOTH MOUNTAIN

Jordan watched carefully as the minister stopped and got down on his knees. His canine companion sauntered up beside him and sat, alert. Jordan could hear the minister praying under his breath. Though he couldn't quite make out the words, he got the strange suspicion that he was praying for their safety.

Compelled by forces beyond his control, Jordan stepped out from among the brush to make himself known. He waved one hand above his head while placing a lone finger to his lips. He didn't want to alert the creature of their presence, nor did he want to witness the disappearance of anyone else.

The bloodhound whimpered and the minister looked up. A smile of relief fell across his face. "Jordan? What are you doing in there, lad? Come on out!"

"Shhh," Jordan whispered back, motioning for the preacher to join him in the trees. "It's not safe."

The old man waddled over to Jordan's foxhole and put a strong hand on his shoulder. It was much stronger than the younger man would've expected, like a sturdy oak amongst flimsy pines.

"How did you find me?"

"You left the markers on the path, and then your footprints led this way," the minister replied, searching for Jordan's traveling companion. "Are you alright? Where is Deon?"

The cracked dam could hold no longer. Jordan broke

down into tears. He couldn't help it. It was all too much. The day had been a disaster, but more than that, he had lost his truest friend. The young man fell to his knees and wept. Unintelligible whispers escaped his stuttering lips. Though he tried, he couldn't speak, and soon he stopped trying altogether.

Gracious as he was, Reverend Jude knelt beside Jordan. He placed a warm hand on the young man's back and addressed him calmly. "Jordan, I must know what happened here," he said softly. "Evening is almost upon us, and the light is our only ally on the mountain."

After a few breaths, Jordan recounted their perils. He told the minister everything. He explained the strange sound and how they followed it into the forest. He detailed their fear as they escaped into the cave, hiding among the pictographs. He recounted the warnings from those who lived beneath the mountain for centuries, and his failure to heed them. All this before admitting the unforgivable, that he left his best friend behind as a monster from within the mountain chased him out.

His story sounded crazy, of that there was no doubt. In his hysterics, Jordan couldn't help but tell the truth, the whole truth, and nothing but the truth. So help him God, he needed to get it all out. He needed to confess.

The Reverend listened intently to every word. He didn't interrupt, nor did he seem to disbelieve the young man's story. He merely nodded when appropriate and oc-

THE BEAST OF BEAR-TOOTH MOUNTAIN

casionally patted his furry friend, whom he referred to as Scout. He did all this while also dressing Jordan's wound. It seemed as if he took acute mental notes so as to draw up a battle plan. Though, maybe that was just how Jordan was reading it. After all, that's what Deon would've done.

"It's all my fault," Jordan concluded. "If I hadn't been so stupid…" He collected himself before facing the minister. "I know this sounds crazy. I feel like a lunatic, but I swear to you-"

"I believe you, son," Reverend Jude said, rising from the snowy ground. "This has been my life's work, my family's mission. Regrettably, the beast has evaded me for years, and short of plunging into the heart of the mountain myself, I have been unable to vanquish it yet."

"You knew?"

"I did, and I warned you and your friend against ascending the mountain this day. Another week, maybe two, and it may have been safe, but now is the worst time of year."

"What is it?"

"A Nephilim. A mighty warrior born from an unholy mixture of the mortal and the divine. It is not a creature to be trifled with. It knows only violence, only war, and it suffers no remorse."

"And it's what…sentient?"

"Oh, yes. It can think just as it can speak. It has every ability that you or I do, in its own way. Which is why we have not much time."

"You think Deon's still alive?" Jordan asked, elated at the news.

"I do," replied the Reverend.

"Why?"

"This creature rarely entertains houseguests. When its kind ruled these plains, they devoured everything in their path, leaving little behind. But since its brothers fell, this one has resorted to making its meals last. More than likely, your friend will be cooked first. It will keep him alive as it does it, to savor every fearful flavor. It will kill him only after its first taste of flesh and will save the rest for as long as it can be preserved."

Jordan wasn't sure what to say. He barely believed this thing existed to begin with, and he had seen it–at least he thought he'd seen it–with his own two eyes. Horrified, Jordan barely whispered his last question… "Can it die?"

"Not of old age," the minister replied.

Reverend Jude eyed the mountain and unstrapped the 12-gauge from his back, which he then proceeded to load. For a man of the cloth, he was shockingly competent with firearms. Through all the tears, Jordan hadn't noticed the shotgun until now. Despite having grown up around them, he had never felt particularly comfortable with guns. Though, knowing what was out there, he felt a strange sort of peace in knowing that they'd be able to defend themselves should something else come.

THE BEAST OF BEAR-TOOTH MOUNTAIN

As he studied the minister more carefully, he was even further surprised when he noticed another weapon strapped to his side.

"Nice sword."

The minister nodded as he finished loading the last round. "Thank you, it has been in my family for generations."

"You're not really a preacher, are you?" Jordan asked. "You're, what, a Templar Knight or something?"

The Reverend laughed. "Oh no, the small church you passed today is indeed my parish," he insisted, quickly moving on to more important matters. "Creatures like these only stay dead when beheaded," he continued casually. "This blade is so it does not get back up."

The old man tossed the firearm back over his shoulder and removed his sword. It was a beautiful blade and certainly well-cared for. It looked Medieval in origin, though Jordan wasn't exactly an expert. The preacher examined the blade for a moment as if grading it on its sharpness. Evidently, it passed with flying colors as he returned it silently to its sheath.

"I'm sorry," Jordan said abruptly. He had wanted to apologize from the moment he laid eyes on the small-town pastor but had been afraid up until now. "You tried to warn us, and we... This is all my fault."

The Reverend nodded soulfully at the young man. "You made a grave error, but all mistakes might be forgiven if we only admit to them. I appreciate the apology, but I am not the one who needs to hear those words."

There was nothing Jordan wanted more than to repeat them again to Deon. To plead for his forgiveness and hope beyond all hope that he might be worthy of it. He knew that he wasn't, but he'd settle for his friend's life.

"Now, let us embark on this quest and quell this beast."

"What?" Jordan trembled. "I-I can't. I can't go back in there."

"You can and you will, or cowardice will haunt you your whole life. In our brief time, we all find ourselves in the fire, but it is how we handle the flame that determines the type of men we will be. Who knows, maybe this was the moment for which you were made?"

With that, Reverend Jude took his leave, marching on towards the mountain. Scout followed closely by his side, abandoning Jordan to the cold. The young man glanced through the trees towards the horizon and noted the sun's position in the sky. This was his last chance to make it down before nightfall. It was clear that the minister didn't intend to call for help, but maybe Jordan could convince someone else to follow him up the mountain to rescue an injured hiker.

Who was he kidding? No further aid was coming. This was all he was going to get.

Unable or unwilling to stay behind, Jordan rose to his feet and clenched his fist. He had no other choice. Against

THE BEAST OF BEAR-TOOTH MOUNTAIN

the demons of self-preservation screaming at his soul, he knew that the only way to save it was to venture back into the mountain.

Dead or alive, he had to find his friend, even if he didn't return.

The three of them trekked back up towards the dark cavern that led into the heart of Bear-tooth Mountain. The preacher convinced Jordan to go first so he could lead them to the grotto where he and Deon had first found the bones and encountered the giant. Jordan begrudgingly accepted his role as guide, though noted that Scout could probably do the job just as well.

As they entered the darkness, the preacher handed Jordan a new flashlight to illuminate their path. Finding his courage, the young man led them into the tight quarters and retrieved his own pack as they passed the warnings on the wall. For now, he left Deon's things aside, taking only his nearly empty water bottle for safekeeping.

Jordan kept his gaze forward to avoid locking eyes with the gaping beast at the legend's end. He was no longer ignorant concerning the painted warnings on the wall and now considered them sacred. "It's this way," he whispered. "This tunnel leads right into the cavern. I can show you where the giant came from once we get there."

"Then let us make haste," the preacher replied.

The trio traveled like mice, scurrying through the earth with hardly a sound. Even Scout knew better than to bark or growl, despite the foul odors she was no doubt detecting. All urgency aside, their three-piece caravan was slow-moving. Jordan fought the pain, dreading every step as he drew nearer to the mammoth that haunted his every thought.

Sure, he wanted to rescue Deon. He wanted to save his friend from this terrible fate, a fate ignited because of his own foolishness. He just wished for anyway other way than venturing deeper into the beast's domain. If there was one, he never found it.

"Your leg," said the minister, breaking the silence. "How is it?"

"It's fine," Jordan lied. He didn't want to make a thing of it.

"You should rest."

"I thought we didn't have much time?"

"Stop," the minister said firmly.

Jordan did. The Reverend's order struck him like a private on the first day of boot camp. The elderly minister made his way towards him and knelt down to examine his leg. He felt the preacher's calloused hands touch the wounded area and winced a little at the pain. All he could hear was the Reverend muttering beneath his breath. Jordan couldn't tell what was happening in the dark. He'd kept his light fixed on the floor in front of them to avoid

THE BEAST OF BEAR-TOOTH MOUNTAIN

any surprises, which meant he couldn't see a thing in any other direction. Less than a minute later, Reverend Jude was back on his feet and ready to proceed.

Maybe it was the adrenaline, or maybe the minister's silent prayer, but Jordan's leg felt as good as new. Soon, their pace doubled, as if a new wind had come upon them. Jordan felt lighter, at least physically, and led them faithfully through the last stretch of the tunnel. In moments, they had reached the hollow. The blackened room was nothing but an empty space, but Jordan knew what lay ahead.

Once they reached the tunnel's end, which opened into the grotto, Reverend Jude took the lead. He and Scout scuttled to the nearest boulder and peered into the dark hollow. The coast was clear, at least for now, and he beckoned Jordan to follow him into the open. The minister was handling his shotgun now, alert as a hawk gliding over a river in search of weakened prey. Though the man's poor eyesight might've been a hindrance, he seemed completely calm as Jordan slowly aimed his light ahead.

"Hold it steady, lad," Reverend Jude ordered. "Our eyes need all the help they can get in here."

"Yes sir," Jordan replied. He walked softly behind Scout, who was trailing her master, and only stopped when the bloodhound veered off course. "Umm, Reverend?"

"What is it?"

Jordan redirected his light to Scout. The hound was clearly on a mission of her own and had sauntered only a few meters away. Within seconds, she was already on her way back to them, a lone hiking boot housed in her jaws.

"That's Deon's!" Jordan cried.

"Hush," the old man warned. "We cannot attract any unwanted attention, least of all from a giant."

Jordan's excitement turned instantly to dread. He began to think about Deon's boot, that it might be the only remains discoverable by the end of all this. Yes, the Reverend had said that Deon was likely to be cooked first, preserved only so long as the creature could bear to wait, *but how did he really know that?* Until this morning, he had thought that giants were only real in fairy tales. He'd thought that they were nothing more than childish legends with no rooted basis in history. He had only just discovered that these legends were in fact true.

"What does this mean for Deon?" he whispered back.

"Perhaps it fell off when the creature took him," the Reverend pondered. "Or, a more hopeful interpretation may be that he kicked it off himself, hoping to lead us further in."

That word haunted him. *Hope.* Jordan was trying not to hope, or at least not so much as to be disappointed if things didn't turn out as he hoped. Before today, Jordan had many hopes, but now he could only focus on the task at hand. The present had consumed him so that he could

THE BEAST OF BEAR-TOOTH MOUNTAIN

not bear to even think about the future.

What hope did they have after all this? Would they even make it out alive? This whole expedition was out of control. Who was this preacher to be hunting giants anyway?

A snuff from Scout's nostrils pulled Jordan out of his mental spiral. Those thoughts wouldn't help him now. Self-pity and doubt would get him killed in here. He had to be focused. For Deon.

Having been lost in thought, Jordan hadn't noticed that Scout had taken the lead again, waiting for him to follow before resuming the search. The Reverend gently handed over Deon's boot and they continued on their way.

"Do you have a weapon?" the Reverend asked.

"No," Jordan replied. "I don't think—" He stopped when he remembered the bear spray and quickly retrieved it. He'd wished more than anything that he had Deon's hunting knife, which was probably also hiding in the dirt somewhere. "How's this?"

"That will do," the Reverend replied.

Though Jordan had fought against any outward optimism, it seemed that hope was stirring within him after all. As Scout led the pair across the stream and past the bones, they recovered more of Deon's personal effects. Another boot, some socks, a wristwatch, and even his wallet were all collected by Jordan and carefully stored within his pack.

Hope was arising in his heart as he began to believe that the once-crazed preacher might've been right after all.

It wasn't long before they came upon an open crevice on the other side of the grotto. Unlike the cavern that Jordan and Deon had hidden in hours earlier, this one rounded out like a subway tunnel. Rather than being lined with cold steel and concrete, this darkened waste was a road that no soul wished to travel.

Unfortunately, that was the sole reason they were there.

Not wasting a moment, the Reverend led Jordan and Scout into the new tunnel. It was certainly tall enough for the creature to wander in and out of comfortably, and while the ceiling wasn't quite as high as the previous hollow, Jordan noted how much more convenient this tunnel was. Aside from its height, it was also much wider. The dusty walls rounded upwards as if to give the giant a considerable amount of space, which likewise gave the three of them permission to walk around at arm's length.

On any other day, Jordan might've remarked at the inner beauty of Bear-tooth Mountain, how even here in the darkness it had a sort of primal charm. But today wasn't any other day.

After dozens of twists and turns from that first mountainous ballroom, they put away their flashlights as the Reverend noted a light that flickered at the end of the tunnel. Despite all appearances, this was no heavenly wonder. Dazzling licks danced along the cavern walls as they escaped past another room, one accompanied by inhuman grunts and groans. Jordan gripped his bear spray tight.

"It might not do much against a giant," he thought. "But it's loads better than nothing."

As they watched the light flicker, they smelled the most potent stench they'd ever had the unpleasure of inhaling. Rotten eggs baking on a warm, sunny day would've been a treat by comparison. The funk filled the air and was instantly nauseating. Jordan could smell hints of sulfur within the malodor, though he couldn't quite figure out the primary agent.

"What's that smell?" Jordan asked, pressing his sleeve into his face.

"We are at Death's door," the Reverend replied solemnly. "And that is his signature dish."

The Reverend bid them to halt. Without a sound, he knelt kindly beside Scout and ordered her to "sit" and "stay." She obeyed, of course, and he turned to Jordan with a grave shadow across his face. Jordan had never seen the minister look so grim, and he could hardly guess the type of sermon that was about to be delivered.

"You must take all your fear and surrender it," the preacher spoke firmly. "If you do not, it will be the death of you and your friend."

"What about you?"

"I am prepared for this battle, and I will be with you until the very end if that is our fate. I am not afraid to die."

"That makes one of us," Jordan muttered.

"Jordan, I cannot deliver you from your fear, but there is One who can. If you can trust that, this giant will fall."

"I'm not sure I can," the younger man replied sheepishly.

"You must."

With that, Reverend Jude turned towards the giant's lair and marched to the edge of the opening. Jordan followed close behind as they peered into the stony dungeon. It was large, though not quite as large as the grotto where they had found the human remains. And no water dared trickle through here.

In the very center of the room sat a large fire. The heat from the flames could be felt all the way to the entrance and triumphantly lit up the entire space. Half a dozen columns were scattered about the chamber, measuring upwards of forty feet, well above the creature's own head. Given the size of this hellhole, the columns proved necessary to hold the rest of the mountain at bay.

It didn't take long before Jordan caught glimpses of skeletal remains littered around the giant's home. The bones of nearly every creature known to inhabit the area lay lifelessly around the desecrated mausoleum. From bob-

THE BEAST OF BEAR-TOOTH MOUNTAIN

cats and grizzlies to horned sheep and elk, the cavern floor was littered with casual trophies that marked years of expert-level hunting experience. Somehow, it was worse than the human remains, though that was probably the smell.

It was then that Jordan saw him.

Curled on the floor near one of the farthest pillars was Deon. Jordan was too far away to tell if he was breathing, but he noted the small pools of blood glistening in the firelight beside his friend's bare feet. The flame gifted it a sort of glossy sheen that would no doubt further whet the creature's appetite.

That's right, Deon wasn't alone.

With a rumble, the giant wandered out from behind one of the wider columns across the craggy hellscape. It carried a set of splintered wooden beams and forcibly placed them on either side of the flame. Each pole made its way into a small but deep hole on opposite ends of the fire, sliding in unencumbered. From there, it uncoiled make-shift ropes tied to each post and tossed them to the ground. Jordan wasn't sure what terrified him more, the horrible truth that monsters were indeed real, or that they were just as inventive as men.

Though the beast was more intelligent than the other creatures that made Bear-tooth Mountain their home, it was just as violent. Probably more so. As if dragging a rabbit, the giant grabbed Deon by the legs and pulled him along the uneven ground, his head tossing and turning with each

MICHAEL JOHN PETTY

jagged bump. It retrieved one of the ropes and fastened it around his legs, wrapping them tightly together to stall any possible movement. Deon was beginning to wake now, but before he could so much as gasp, the creature secured the other line around his arms. Deon was too weak to protest.

With all his appendages fettered, the creature hoisted Deon over the fire, pulling the loose ends taut against the poles guarding the inferno. The young man's back was to the fire, which flickered nearly a person's length below him. The beast hadn't considered stripping the human of his clothing, which was fortunate for Deon as the flames began to lick his back. The licks were quick at first, with light repetitive motions, but as each lash grew more intense, the irritating pain soon became unbearable. In no time at all, Deon's screams echoed hopelessly throughout the chamber. Jordan couldn't take it.

"We have to do something," Jordan demanded. "That thing will kill him."

"Quite right," spoke the minister, his shotgun at the ready. "Here is what we will do. Scout and I will distract the creature and lure it away from the flames. You will hide behind that column over there."

"That's it?"

The Reverend looked patiently into Jordan's eyes as if he were a teacher answering a child during Sunday school. "When it has engaged with me, rescue your friend."

Jordan took a deep breath. A familiar chill crept up

THE BEAST OF BEAR-TOOTH MOUNTAIN

his legs, through his lower back, and all the way to the base of his neck. It was that voice again. That voice that nearly convinced him to abandon Deon once before. It was taunting him now, hoping again to make a coward out of him. He didn't want to give in, he didn't want to let his best friend die. Jordan wanted to be brave, brave as the old preacher, but he-

No, not this time.

"Are you with me?" the minister asked.

"Yes," Jordan replied.

"Then go, now. Await my signal."

Before he could change his mind, Jordan slunk into the cursed tomb. The creature's back was turned, preoccupied with sharpening what appeared to be a blade crafted from the humerus of a grizzly. This gave Jordan just enough time to take cover and run through the plan once more. The beast paid no mind to the young grasshopper making his way across the cavern floor, it was too preoccupied savoring the smells of Deon's burning flesh.

Jordan was terrified. He'd never been this close. Not willingly. The heat was more than he could bear. Sweat melted down his back like wax on an over-lit candle. He could hardly breathe as he imagined the giant catching wind of the drumline buried within his chest. His eyes closed as he attempted to steady himself with nervous hands, but it only made it worse.

The creature moved past the flame and took a deep,

guttural breath. It inhaled the horrid aromas as it circled its beaten prey. For a moment, it seemed to wander toward the exit, but it soon found its way back to its main course.

Though he tried to ignore them, Deon's screams pierced Jordan's soul. He felt powerless. *What am I doing?* Jordan asked himself. But deep down he knew. He wouldn't know peace until Deon was safe, and the creature was dead.

He turned to the old preacher and exchanged small nods. It was time.

The Reverend let slip a smile before marching confidently into the cavern. His awesome battle cry echoed throughout the ceilings and nearly rumbled across the floor. The giant was surprised, it wasn't excepting company. Greeting its guest, it let out only a short snarl before the Reverend forcefully interrupted. Slug after slug burrowed itself deep within the creature's thick hide as the minster shot the beast like it was the broad side of a worn-down barn. One blast after another pierced the creature, which wiped its blood angrily to the floor.

Jordan was floored. He'd never look at a minister the same way again, and he certainly wouldn't judge one by their seemingly crazy ramblings. The way Reverend Jude battled the beast was unlike anything he'd ever seen. He even avoided friendly fire by putting himself between Deon and the giant.

After five shells, the Reverend stopped to reload. "Now, girl!" he yelled as Scout leaped into action. She had

THE BEAST OF BEAR-TOOTH MOUNTAIN

refrained from attacking the monster while her master was blasting holes into its chest but had barked up a mean storm in the interim. Though, the creature didn't give the faithful hound much thought.

Instead, it charged at the preacher, its jagged grizzly-bone blade in hand.

Only two shells in, Reverend Jude threw himself out of the way as the creature cut through nothing but air, waving its oak-like arms past the spot where the preacher's head once rested.

Three shells now.

Jordan watched as the creature turned back to its prey, foaming at the mouth. It had never experienced a home invasion before, at least not for centuries. Its pale eyes grew dark as it emitted an ungodly sound that would've been enough to bust an eardrum had the Reverend or Scout been any closer. Jordan could see the blood trickling down the beast's hairy back but stifled his excitement. He couldn't risk being discovered.

Four shells loaded.

The Reverend called it good. He blasted another round into the beast's chest, hailing it with names like "abomination" and "hybrid filth." The preacher didn't take too kindly to the creature, almost as if he took its very existence personally. As a result, he unloaded decades—no, generations of pent-up righteous fury into its unclean flesh.

The giant gasped as it glanced down at its blood-stained

chest. It touched the red ooze seeping from its torso and carefully brought the ichor to its lips. The taste of its own blood seemed to drive it mad as it charged at the pastor with reddened eyes. The Reverend dodged another swipe as the giant plunged its weapon into one of the pillars on the opposite end of the chamber. The makeshift blade snapped in two and the sharper edge pierced the giant's forearm.

It cried out in agony as it ripped the bloody bony blade out of its forearm and tossed it to the ground. The minister took the time to reload as the creature held its damaged arm in disarray. Jordan was thankful that it seemed confused, but that confusion was soon replaced by pure rage.

The Reverend called Scout back to his side. Before making it there, she plunged her short canines into the giant's oversized toe, giving the preacher just enough time to fire two more rounds into the beast.

Furious, the giant snatched the Reverend up with its good hand and brought him near its doubled rows of teeth. The monster began to crush him with its enormous fingers as it grimaced a crooked smile. Though he struggled under the pressure, the minister fired another blast in return, driving buckshot straight into the monster's forehead. The giant shook violently as it snarled, clawing through the pain. It winced and writhed as it fought the itch. Jordan watched helplessly as the Reverend held on for dear life. He prayed that the creature's pain was enough to keep it from squeezing the minister any tighter.

THE BEAST OF BEAR-TOOTH MOUNTAIN

Within seconds, the giant fell with a thud that rivaled the largest oak. It wasn't a pleasant fall, nor was it long-winded. The moment the creature hit the ground the cavern rumbled. For a moment, Jordan had forgotten all about Deon's merciless cries, thinking only about the welfare of the preacher.

Moments passed before the minister found the strength to claw his way out of the giant's grip. He rubbed his eyes and uttered a quick prayer of thanks before spotting Jordan watching from afar.

"Go!" Reverend Jude shouted.

Wasting no more time, Jordan hopped from column to column until he was beside the creature's home oven. The heat was excruciating, more like a country bonfire than your average backyard grill. He glanced up at Deon who was suspended nearly six feet in the air and couldn't imagine the pain he was experiencing. His pants had darkened, and his jacket blistered. Jordan noted the singed hair on the back of his even redder neck.

There wasn't much time to spare.

Jordan attempted to untie his friend. The bonds proved tremendously tight and would be impossible to loosen on his own. He searched quickly for another sharpened bone, hoping the creature had left some extra crumbs behind. Nothing. He was hopeless, he didn't even have a small pocketknife to help. The preacher had a blade, maybe he could use that…

And that's when he saw it. The one object Jordan hadn't thought to bring.

It was Deon's hunting knife.

The blade was stained with blood–which Jordan hoped was the giant's–but was otherwise intact. He retrieved it and carefully began sawing his way through the cord that held Deon's legs above the ground. Even with the knife, the bonds proved extremely temperamental. They were coarse and splintered in ways that cut Jordan's hands as he unraveled them. But after a minute or two, the bonds came loose.

Jordan hadn't anticipated that cutting the rope would send Deon straight into the fire, but he recognized his error just in time to catch his friend by the toes. The thought of being captured by the giant had been enough to haunt his every waking thought, but nearly burning Deon alive would've been infinitely worse. Using all his strength, Jordan hoisted Deon upwards and around the flame before gently resting his blistered body against the opposite post. Thankfully, most of his clothing was still intact.

"Deon! Deon, wake up!" Jordan shook his friend but got no response. "Come on…" He checked his pulse. It was weak, but he was still there. "Deon, please. I need you to wake up."

Still nothing. Jordan was running out of options now. He glanced over at the minister to see him slowly carving through the giant's massive neck with his ancient sword. It

THE BEAST OF BEAR-TOOTH MOUNTAIN

would take much longer to slice through the creature than it took to cut the rope around Deon's hands. He turned back to Deon and got to work at freeing his wrists. Within moments, he'd broken through, and Deon lay still against the post.

"I'm so sorry about this…" Jordan sighed and then slapped Deon as hard as he could across the face. His hand made a clapping sound against Deon's cheek that seemed to echo throughout the chamber. The Reverend even turned to take a look. Somehow, it worked, and Deon's glazed eyes rolled open.

"Wha–wh're'm I?" Deon said, barely getting the words out.

"Don't worry," Jordan responded. "Everything's going to be okay."

"Wh're izzit?"

Jordan glanced over at the giant's lifeless body. Scout stood still beside her master as Reverend Jude continued his gruesome work. This was going to take a while.

"It's dead," Jordan said softly.

His eyes fell back on Deon who looked as if he'd gone nine rounds in the ring with the Italian Stallion. He was barely breathing. Each uneasy breath came with a throaty wheeze that sounded even more painful than the burns on his back.

"You're gonna be okay, Deon," Jordan said, reassuring himself more than anyone. "I'm so sorry."

85

MICHAEL JOHN PETTY

"What fer?" Deon coughed. His voice was coming back to him, though it was still a bit hoarse.

"All of this. If I hadn't insisted on exploring the cave…"

"I-I wanted to follow…the sound," Deon interrupted.

"Yeah, but I pushed it too far. You were freaked and I didn't take any of it seriously. I didn't take *you* seriously."

Deon forced a smile. "All that…matterssiss…we're okay."

Jordan nodded, though he still couldn't help but feel responsible. Hoping to avoid Deon's pitiful gaze, he turned back towards the old man and his dog. As the minister struggled to hack through the giant's throat, something strange caught his eye. Given the circumstances, Jordan had thought that the creature was dead, but unbeknownst to the minister, its fingers had begun to twitch.

"Uh, Reverend?" Jordan said. The Reverend didn't respond, so he repeated himself, louder this time. "Reverend?"

As Jordan called out, the fingers slowly formed into a fist. Before the minister could notice, a sharp screech rang from the giant's throat.

The monster's log-ish arm launched the pastor across the room. Jordan could hardly believe his eyes as the giant stumbled back to its feet, the large gash from the base of its neck spilling buckets of blood down its chest. It might have been a trick of the light, or maybe the preacher hadn't gotten as deep as he thought, but Jordan could swear that the dent in his neck was slowly contracting all on its own.

THE BEAST OF BEAR-TOOTH MOUNTAIN

The monster snarled as it eased toward the fallen preacher, its rigid claws primed for the kill.

Scout jumped in the gap. The brave bloodhound bit the giant, her teeth sinking deep into its grisly palm. Scout was growling something fierce. The creature seemed unable to feel the handful of little knives seeping into its skin. To the giant, Scout's efforts were nothing more than the bit of a small insect. It effortlessly swiped her across the room, straight into the jagged wall nearest the chamber's exit.

"Reverend! Get up!" Jordan screamed, though he soon wished he hadn't. His cry had caught the attention of the giant, who reared its ugly scowl towards the young men crouched beside the fire. It snarled at the pair as it redirected all its fury toward them.

Having come back to his senses, the Reverend reached for his firearm. "Abomination!"

The beast glanced back just in time to get another face full of buckshot, which erupted a fresher gush of blood and guts and missing teeth. The monster cried out, though Jordan couldn't tell if it was in pain or anger. The fact that the beast was still standing was incredible. He's never heard of anything like it, not even in the animal kingdom. Rage served as the creature's only lifeblood now, and it had more than enough to spare.

Wasting no more time, Jordan pulled Deon to his feet. "Can you walk?"

Deon's head bobbled around in what Jordan could

only hope was a nod and so he quickly removed Deon's boots from his pack. Jordan fastened them onto Deon's blooded and bare feet before they shoved off, darting behind each darkened pillar as the giant tussled endlessly with the minister.

The creature barreled towards the clergyman—who had slowly made his way to the exit—as more metal fragments rained into its already deformed face. Unable to see out of its blood-soaked eyes, the giant scrambled aimlessly about its chambers. It crashed into boulders and stomped on animal carcasses as it stumbled in a frightened rage. It nearly trampled Jordan and Deon as they passed between the last two columns.

"This way!" the Reverend hollered. "Quickly!"

The boys scrambled over to the old man with Jordan taking the brunt of the weight. The creature must've heard them as it turned towards their frantic steps and followed closely after. Whether by accident or advent, Jordan stumbled over a lion skull, and they toppled to the ground. The creature stepped right over them and continued headfirst through one of the cavern's various support columns, knocking the pillar out of place. Bits of dust showered from the ceiling, though not one of them took notice.

At once, the Reverend was by the boy's side and silently helped them back to their feet. He led them quickly and quietly out the chamber's exit and leaned Deon against the stony outer wall.

THE BEAST OF BEAR-TOOTH MOUNTAIN

"We must leave, now," the minister ordered.

"You don't… Hav'ta tell me twice," Deon muttered.

"What about Scout?" Jordan insisted.

"I will retrieve her," the Reverend whispered, glancing back into the cavern. She was hurt, badly, but he wouldn't leave her here to die.

Jordan peered around the corner of the chamber's outer wall to see the giant slowly push itself off the ground. It snarled as it pawed at its bloody face, trying desperately to dig the shells out of its tattered flesh. If they had been anywhere else but beside its own dingy chambers, the giant may have been able to smell them, but since the entire room reeked of death, sound was its only ally.

It was then that Jordan spotted the minister's blood-stained sword. It lay still on the ground about twenty feet from the creature on the opposite side of the chamber from Scout. It called to him in the firelight, but its message was interrupted when the Reverend darted back into the giant's lair.

Jordan watched as the minister scooped up his furry companion as delicately and quietly as he could. He was careful to take slow but firm steps and even shorter breaths until he got to her. But all the preacher's efforts were for naught. The moment he picked her up, Scout whimpered at the pain, and one could hardly blame her. Instantly, this caught the giant's unfocused attention, and while the creature still couldn't see through its dried and bloody eyes, its

MICHAEL JOHN PETTY

enormous ears pointed it in the right direction.

Instantly, the monster sped towards the Reverend and Scout, blood and sweat oozing from its face. Taking advantage of its disability, the minister escaped its charge without so much as a scratch as the giant rammed itself head-first into the nearest cavern wall. A rumbling shot through the cavern and a quake moved like lightning across the ceiling, which spit more dust onto the floor. It wouldn't be long now before this hollow wasn't so hollow anymore.

The Reverend stumbled back to his feet with Scout still in his arms. Bloodied and bruised, he limped back towards the exit as the creature hollered in agony. It was distraught, not to mention furious. Nothing could calm its rage nor keep it from finding its prey now. As the minister hobbled along, it crept up behind him like an uneasy shadow. Though it couldn't see the preacher, it heard the panting of his breath and the cracking of his knees as he fled the depths of Hell.

All Jordan could do was watch helplessly. Or maybe that's what he told himself. No, he was no longer the scared boy who left his friends to die. He was something else now.

At least, he wanted to be.

Jordan lunged back into the heart of the cavern. He didn't think, prepare, or weigh the options, he just jumped. "Hey!" he screamed at the creature. "Over here!"

The creature turned its head like an owl, and its body followed suit. It snorted in a burst of hot air, followed by

THE BEAST OF BEAR-TOOTH MOUNTAIN

an exhale of blood and pus and guts.

Jordan didn't waste time. He ran to the nearest support column and pounded on it with his bare hands. "You don't want them! Come get me!"

The giant abandoned his pursuit of the Reverend and committed itself fully to Jordan's demise. Out of its double-rowed jaws escaped another ungodly screech, a familiar sound Jordan wished that he and Deon had never heard in the first place. The creature had entertained its unwelcomed guests long enough and had worked up a hearty appetite.

The giant fought through the pain and sprinted at Jordan, giving the young man only seconds to hurdle himself from the target zone. Like clockwork, the creature crashed with its entire momentum into the next support column, blowing it apart like a set of Lincoln Logs. The collapse started a series of tremors that were worse than before. Rock and dirt like hail fell from above, and the dust obscured everyone's vision. If the giant's lair wasn't safe before, they were in even more danger now.

When he came to, Jordan was face-first on the ground. His ears were ringing from the crash, and his head spun as if he'd been clocked himself. He hadn't, but he knew that he'd be feeling that in the morning.

If they made it that long.

As he looked up from the dusty ground and wiped a mixture of sweat and grime from his forehead, a shimmer caught his eye. The auburn flicker waved side to side in

91

front of him, like tree branches in the wind. It was beautiful, the most beautiful thing he'd seen thus far in the mountain. But it wasn't a flicker at all, only the reflection of one. He noticed a sharp edge that gave off a distinct sheen of its own, and it was then that he realized the preacher's sword was lying before him.

Before he knew what was happening, the blade was already in his hand. He suddenly felt the courage to climb back to his feet and face the beast once more. As he did, the world came back to him, and he heard the distant cries of the Reverend and Deon as they pleaded with him to retreat. Though he couldn't quite make out their words, he could tell that they were warning him of something.

Jordan looked back at the beast lying still on the ground. The creature was covered with the remains of the rocky column and struggled to shake them off.

It was then that Jordan almost died.

BAM! A massive boulder landed only a few feet away from him. Had he not climbed back to his feet, he may have been crushed. Jordan looked upward to see that the ceiling was beginning to give way. His escape window was closing fast.

Suddenly, the monster pushed itself back to its feet. The creature had gone from a ghostly pale to a more colorful black and blue, with blood-red stains all over. A soft growl hardly escaped its misshapen lips, which were ripped up like used pieces of cardboard in a wet dumpster.

THE BEAST OF BEAR-TOOTH MOUNTAIN

It wasn't going to make it.

Faster than a rabbit during open season, Jordan turned back to the exit–sword still in hand–and ran like hell. As the earthen roof collapsed around him, Jordan dodged the debris like a man possessed. Never in his wildest dreams would he have thought he could run like that, but he knew that if he thought any more about it, he'd be pummeled by the earth from above. So he kept running, and he didn't look back.

The creature stumbled behind him, pelted by boulders and rocks and dirt and dust as it attempted its own escape. Each new hit slowed its pace until it finally couldn't press on any longer. The giant was crushed by the enormous weights placed upon it and was soon buried deep beneath the dust. The innards of Bear-tooth Mountain filled the giant's chambers, which had now become its tomb.

The chalky air filled Jordan's lungs as he thrust himself out into the tunnel. Deon, Reverend Jude, and Scout had moved back to avoid any fallout, and the moment Jordan was clear, the minister hauled him further in. As the final pillars gave way, the hollow was overcome by earth and dust. The firelight was fully extinguished, and they were all left aimless in the dark.

Somehow, Jordan had made it out alive. He couldn't believe it either, but it was true. The creature was gone,

Deon was safe, and they had all escaped the banquet Death had rightfully prepared for them. It didn't feel real, let alone possible, and yet there they were. Broken and bruised, there was no doubt about that, but with enough breath in their lungs to keep on.

In the cloud of darkness, Deon had found and lit the preacher's flashlight. He leaned weak against the wall but still fought to make himself useful. The Reverend had set Scout aside so that he might properly tend to the younger men, and ever since, the bloodhound whimpered in hopes of not being forgotten. Thankfully, her master was just as faithful as she.

Still clutching the Reverend's sword, Jordan stood as still as the mountain itself. He was in shock, though he couldn't begin to comprehend it. He began to question whether he had made it out alive at all or if he was about to be ushered into eternity. Maybe he was a ghost? A phantom, given one last chance to commune with the living. If he were dead, this didn't look anything like Heaven. If there even was such a thing. Though, now that he knew that giants–which were once bound by the pages of folktales and D&D manuals–were indeed flesh-and-blood monsters, how dare he believe otherwise?

"I suppose not running with scissors was a lesson your mother failed to teach you," the minister said through his overly dusted lips. Jordan didn't offer back a quip. He just stood there; eyes glazed as far back as they could go. The

THE BEAST OF BEAR-TOOTH MOUNTAIN

minister put a careful hand on the young man's shoulder. "Jordan, you can let go now."

"We're–We're alive…" Jordan stuttered.

"By grace alone," the minister rejoiced. "But we are all a little worse for wear, I am afraid."

Jordan glanced down at his hands, still gripping Reverend Jude's birthright like a safety bar on a rollercoaster. He shook off the embarrassment and offered it back to its master.

"You dropped this," Jordan said.

The minister didn't say a word. He held up a hand in silent protest and unbuckled the sheath from his belt. "Hold it for me," the Reverend said, handing the casing over. His command was disguised as a friendly request. "With Scout in my arms, it would be best if I did not have to worry about anything else."

Jordan didn't argue and clipped the sheath onto his person. But before he slid the blade back into its place, he remembered the old stories of knights and kings and took a moment to wipe each side of the brand along his sleeve. While the blade wasn't spotless, it was the best job he could do given the circumstances.

The Reverend seemed to approve, and it was then that Jordan noticed that the preacher's shotgun was also missing. He must've dropped it in all that commotion. Unlike the sword, it wasn't irreplaceable, but it reminded Jordan of a brand that was.

MICHAEL JOHN PETTY

"Here," Jordan said as he handed Deon back his father's hunting knife. It had somehow made its way into Jordan's jacket pocket and miraculously hadn't betrayed him while he was distracting the gigantic creature. "It had some blood on it."

"It's not mine," Deon muttered, holding it tight. "I didn't go down...without a fight, you know."

Jordan smiled. "Your pack is still in the tunnel. We can grab it on our way out."

Deon agreed. He was breathing easy now that the creature was gone. He couldn't believe that he was standing, well, leaning there in the flesh. Sure, he was missing a few cuts of flesh, and he could still feel the heat on his back and neck, but everything else seemed intact.

More than that, he couldn't believe that Jordan had returned to rescue him. He had been the most unlikely person to throw himself into the fire for another—a phrase that now held new meaning for them both.

"Th-thank you," Deon said. "For coming back for me."

"Yeah, well..." Jordan stumbled over his words. He looked to the minister for aid, though the old man seemed preoccupied with dressing Scout's wounds. He had done more than enough anyway. "I wouldn't have forgiven myself if I had left you to die. I couldn't."

Deon slid his blade back into his belt loop and smiled. "A lot of that going around."

THE BEAST OF BEAR-TOOTH MOUNTAIN

"Yeah," Jordan said. "It was the least I could do."

Having been eavesdropping on their exchange, the minister scooped Scout back up in his arms. He, for one, was ready for the journey home. "Are you boys ready?"

They nodded. They couldn't have been more ready to leave this place. After years of dreaming about reaching the summit of Bear-tooth Mountain, their appetite for adventure had been thoroughly quenched. If they never saw the innards of the mountain again, they'd die happy men. Jordan adjusted his pack and offered Deon a hand, pulling the wounded warrior back to his feet.

Within minutes they had left the giant's tomb to its bitter decay. Jordan helped Deon along as Reverend Jude followed a few paces behind them. Jordan had at first tried to hold the light in front of them so that Deon didn't stumble, but soon delegated the task to Deon, who was itching to help.

It was much harder for Jordan to support Deon along than the other way around. He was panting and sweating profusely, more than he had even while distracting the creature. Each step felt agonizing, but they had little choice. He couldn't imagine how the Reverend felt, carrying Scout all by himself. The old man was certainly suffering, though he didn't complain even once. And now that she had been tended to, Scout didn't much either.

Jordan pressed on through the subway-like tunnel, leading their caravan back to the open grotto. He didn't have much energy left, and the group didn't have hardly any food or water to sustain themselves either.

What they did have, they quickly shared. It would have to be enough to tie everyone over for a while, though Jordan was nervous that they wouldn't make it back before Deon passed out. Hopefully, he wouldn't keel over on the way back down, or succumb to any internal injuries that they didn't know about. He prayed the fresh air would make all the difference.

The group scuttled through the widened tunnel, with nothing but the crunch of their footsteps to keep their ears company. They didn't say much during this time, content that the battle and rescue had said more than enough. They were exhausted anyhow–if that word could even begin to cover it–and so they continued to march forward, speaking only through short grunts and heavy groans.

It wasn't long before they made it through the tunnel and back into the open hollow. The same one with the dusty bones and the flowing stream. When bypassing the human remains, Jordan couldn't help but dwell on their near fate. They too nearly ended up like these nameless, and mostly faceless, bones on the floor. Had it not been for the preacher, they would've been dead.

Upon hearing the trickle of the still, small stream, Deon could hardly contain himself. He nearly leaped out

THE BEAST OF BEAR-TOOTH MOUNTAIN

of Jordan's arms to crawl into the life-giving waters, lapping them up like a dog.

The trio filled up their receptacles with as much water as they could carry and chugged it then and there. After pulling him out of the water and setting him aside to rest, Jordan and Reverend Jude were sure to give Deon as much as he asked for. He drank nearly an entire bottle's worth in two minutes and still wanted more. Scout drank her fair share also, and they were all as content as they possibly could be.

Jordan helped Deon alongside a stalagmite, giving him some much-needed support. He took a palm of water from the stream and poured it down the base of his neck. The cool elixir trickled down his spine and eased some of the stabbing pain that ran intermittently up and down his entire body. Though they seemed much closer to Hell, it felt more like Heaven.

The Reverend had also taken a seat beside the stream. He pet Scout softly, stroking slowly down her back as she lazily lapped in a puddle beside the rill. He hadn't mentioned it to the others, but he was beginning to feel a weakness in his knees. Now that the excitement was over, he was devolving back into the old man he was used to being. Though he had made it a habit of hiking the mountain with rigorous consistency, battling such a vicious creature was as draining as running a marathon in the middle of the harshest winter. He was beat.

MICHAEL JOHN PETTY

He stopped petting Scout for a moment to crack the stiff fingers on his left hand. One by one he cracked them, and each snap echoed throughout the earthen hall. As his ring finger cracked, Jordan noticed for the first time the gold band wrapped tightly around it. It wasn't anything special, just solid gold molded into a ring the exact size of the old man's finger. It was plain, but it fit him just right.

"Are you married, Reverend?" Jordan asked.

"Yes, I am," the Reverend replied. "Well, I was."

"I'm sorry," Jordan said, wishing he hadn't asked.

"There is no need to be. Like any faithful husband, I mourned her when she passed, but I am reminded that her death was not in vain. She has gone on to be with our Lord and King now, and I will no doubt meet her there shortly myself."

"Still, it must be hard," Jordan said. He had never known that sort of love. He'd been interested in a few girls in college, but he never found the right time to make his move. But after a day like today, anything seemed possible.

"There are days, yes. It can be quite lonely. Though Scout does her best to keep me company. I suppose there are many days when I miss Janet dearly. We had been married almost fifty years before she passed. We were high school sweethearts, the two of us. Romancing her was one of the greatest joys of my life."

"Do you have any kids?" Deon asked.

The minister nodded. "A son, yes. He lives a few towns

THE BEAST OF BEAR-TOOTH MOUNTAIN

over. He is a man of the land, as they say."

"You said your family has guarded this mountain for generations…" Jordan began.

"I did. Yes."

"So, what about your son? Was he supposed to take over one day?"

Reverend Jude leaned back as if he was about to tell the most fantastical tale of adventure. A soft smile crept across his face as his hand swayed back and forth along Scout's back, her bloodied fur gliding between his weary fingers.

"My ancestors were farmers," he began. "Peaceful Protestants who wished only to make a better life for themselves and their families. It was a hard journey west, one full of hardship and suffering." He paused for a moment. "But there was joy too. When they finally settled in this land, the harvest was great. They had a hand in building the town of Carmel from the ground up and were deeply respected within the community." The minister leaned forward now, a serious gloom hovering across his face.

"But come the following spring, they swiftly uncovered the secrets of the mountain. Wishing to be rid of the curse, many died in their attempts to slay the beast. Before this land was granted statehood, my great, great, grandfather vowed that the creature would be slain in four generations. When my father passed, it fell on me to guard this mountain and hunt the abomination myself." He leaned

101

back again as if to signify that the horrors were over.

"My son knows the dangers of these lands, as well as our family history, but I have kept him and his children away from the task. It was *my* destiny to see to it that the creature met its end. Before today, I had only encountered it sparingly, and each time it evaded death." The preacher took a deep breath and exhaled with a holy satisfaction. "Today, you have helped me take back our land and honor my ancestors by witnessing the giant's destruction first-hand. I owe you a great debt."

"So, what are you gonna do now?" Jordan asked.

The Reverend meditated on the question for a moment. He wasn't one who was quick to speak, and though he had an idea of what life might look like in a post-giant world, he had never considered what *his* life would look like.

"I will continue what I have always done," he finally said with conviction. "I will care for the sheep that God has gifted me and enjoy the remaining years I have left with my family."

That was as satisfying an answer as any. Jordan and Deon had no further questions, at least for now. They were all weary, and the Reverend didn't have much else to say either. So, to their surprise, he sang it instead.

O Lord, by thee delivered,
I'll thee with songs extol;

THE BEAST OF BEAR-TOOTH MOUNTAIN

My foes thou hast not suffered,
To glory o'er my fall.
O Lord my God, I sought thee,
And thou didst heal and save;
Thou, Lord, from death didst ransom,
And keep me from the grave.

His holy name remember;
Ye saints, Jehovah praise;
His anger lasts a moment,
His favor all our days.
For sorrow, like a pilgrim,
May tarry for the night;
But joy the heart will gladden,
When dawns the morning light.

In prosp'rous days, I boasted,
Unmoved I shall remain;
For, Lord, thou by thy favor,
My mountain didst maintain.
I soon was sorely troubled,
For thou didst hide thy face;
I cried to thee, Jehovah,
I sought Jehovah's grace.

What can my blood avail thee,
When in the grave I dwell?

Should dust repeat thy praises?
Thy truth and glory tell?
O Lord, on me have mercy,
And my petition hear;
That thou mayst be my helper,
In mercy, Lord, appear.

Jordan and Deon were enamored by the minister's tune. His praises rang deep throughout the earthen walls and rippled across the drifting stream. It was as if somehow the psalm had sanctified the place and breathed into it new life. They sat quietly and listened as the minister sang his ancient hymn. It was beautiful, and they soaked it in.

As he harmonized, Reverend Jude wore his righteous soul on his sleeve. Though, he would've insisted that any righteousness he might've had didn't come from within. It strictly came from without.

After the Reverend finished his song, it was time to move on. They had regained as much of their strength as they were going to and were anxious to leave this cavern behind forever. As they packed up their things, they refreshed themselves in the brook once more, taking in all the savory elixir they could. The minister prepared Scout for travel as Jordan made sure Deon's boots were back on tight. He'd removed them to run his scarred feet through the stream

THE BEAST OF BEAR-TOOTH MOUNTAIN

but had trouble getting them back on again.

"Come on, push," Jordan said.

"I'm trying," Deon insisted.

A moment later, Deon's boots were back on. Jordan laced them up tight and pulled his friend back to his feet. They were about ready to leave when... CRASH!

A booming sound echoed from the massive tunnel they'd traveled from. The group turned and peered into the darkness as if waiting for something to escape from the shadows. They saw nothing but black, though they heard continued crashes bounce throughout the hollow halls.

"It's probably just still caving in, right?" Deon asked, his hand shook with each new crash and thud.

"No time to speculate," Reverend Jude insisted. "We must get you lads out of here immediately."

With haste, the group crossed the stream one by one. They trudged through the grotto toward the smaller crevice that led them into the larger cavern. As they hurried, a sharpened shriek came from the darkness. It was higher than those they'd heard before, and a bit shriller. The longer they stood there, the louder it got. It was nearly impossible to move with such a deafening sound penetrating their ears. Soon, the ground rumbled around them, leading to an even more awful truth.

The creature was not dead after all.

Whether it was the preacher's hymn or just a matter of time, the giant was awake and angrier than ever. If it could

MICHAEL JOHN PETTY

claw its way out of its own tomb, then it was already well on their trail. With how they stank, it could surely smell them as plain as an elk carcass in the heat of the day. There were no rotting corpses to mask their scents here.

They stumbled up the slippery incline as Jordan brought up the rear. He was in the best shape of the bunch, and he wanted to be sure that at least Deon and Scout made it through. They were easy prey now, and though he wasn't a master swordsman by any stretch, he wanted to offer as much protection as he could grant them. There was a small comfort in knowing that the blade was at his disposal. Not that he really knew how to use it.

Behind them, they heard a clawing on the cavern walls followed by another large crash as the creature clumsily bashed itself into each and every obstacle in its way. Jordan turned for only a moment and shone his light across the stream. The beam glared directly into the giant's blood-stained eyes as the beast let out another deafening shriek.

Now that it was in the same room as them, the sound was crippling.

Jordan looked forward as the minister disappeared within the tight cavern that led back to the crevice that he and Deon had hidden in hours earlier. At this point, it might've been days ago for all Jordan knew, but that didn't matter now. One thing he did know was that the giant was too large to be a threat to them if they were inside.

Deon crawled up the slippery slab towards the tunnel.

THE BEAST OF BEAR-TOOTH MOUNTAIN

The shriek had been too much for him and he'd fallen to the ground trying to drag himself forward. He was panting heavier than Scout as sweat melted off his charred neck. He had no desire to lay eyes on that thing ever again. Even if it were to overtake him here, he'd rather not see it coming. As quickly as his arms let him, Jordan pushed Deon forward. It had somehow been easier to carry Deon than to push him, but he didn't have to for long. From the safety of the tunnel, Reverend Jude offered Deon a hand and was instantly pulled inside.

Shoving his friend into the preacher's arms, Jordan stood at the foot of his salvation. It was still too tight to force himself through, so he could only wait until they shuffled further in. Standing there, he could hear the giant's footsteps. Every few rumbles, it either tripped over a boulder or crashed into another column. Although it could smell them clearly, its nose was useless in avoiding the rock formations that had existed within Bear-tooth Mountain for centuries.

Instinctively, Jordan drew the preacher's sword. If he was confident of anything, it was that this would be the final stand. Of whom, he could not say. Likely, the giant would overpower him here. It certainly had the advantage of being a few extra persons high and as strong as a tank. But it was wounded. Angry. It barely knew where it was, and hardly seemed to think straight, let alone care.

If there was ever a moment where Jordan felt he could

win, it was this one. The odds were surely stacked against him, but somehow he knew it to be true.

Within seconds, the creature stood before him. Foaming at the mouth, it knew it had finally cornered its prey and was anxious to savor the kill. What it didn't know was that its prey was thinking the same thing.

Without a sound, Jordan gritted his teeth, raised his sword, and charged.

Deon had blocked Reverend Jude in as the minister helped the injured young man into the safety of the thinning tunnel. Stepping backward, he was careful to avoid Scout, who he'd placed on the floor, and shooed her aside to let him pass. Aided by the vexed minister, Deon fell into the safety of the cavern. He breathed heavily, and then realized something terrible: he could no longer feel Jordan's hands on his back or hear his short breath upon his neck. His friend was still out there.

"Jordan!" Deon screamed, fighting to go back.

"No," the minister said, stifling his own fears. "You are of no use to him like this. You would only end up dead! The creature is no longer hunting for food, it is coursing for revenge."

"Then we can't leave him!"

Reverend Jude didn't answer Deon's plea. He held the withered young man tightly, not giving an inch. The

THE BEAST OF BEAR-TOOTH MOUNTAIN

preacher let loose a simple prayer. It wasn't much, nor was it weighted down by King James language or lofty theological terms. It was simple. The sort of prayer that is prayed when there's nothing else to pray. When all hope feels lost. When darkness creeps in and there isn't a sliver of light to be found.

"Help."

They stood silently in the dark, their flashlights either busted or forgotten in the commotion. There was nothing more to be done. Nothing more to say. Nothing at all. Nothing but waiting. Waiting for either another gut-wrenching screech from the monstrous creature, or some perilous scream from their companion.

The minister realized too late that he might've pinned Deon against the wall and stolen past him to aid Jordan, but given Deon's penchant for throwing himself back into the fire, he discerned that staying put with his arms tight around the injured traveler was where he was meant to be.

The darkness betrayed nothing to them. They could only hear the battle ensuing. The creature snarled at its prey and grunted as it crashed into stony walls and pillars. They heard Jordan cry out in pain but before they could despair, the giant reciprocated with a bawl of its own.

While they could see nothing at first, there were occasional flashes of light that teased them in the dark. They soon recognized it to be the flashlight Jordan had been carrying, and they hoped that it was aiding him in battle.

Another high-pitched shriek filled the innards of Bear-tooth Mountain. Had it been a higher pitch, if that were even possible, it might've caused an avalanche or another quake. Deon nearly fell to his knees covering his ears before the Reverend caught him. From behind him, the minister could hear Scout groaning in pain as she shuffled herself closer to the exit.

An earth-shaking crash followed as the wail died down. The floor thundered, but just as soon as the rumble began again, it ceased. Like the calm before the storm, or maybe the moment right after the storm, a haunting silence fell upon them.

Deon and the Reverend didn't know what to do. If the creature was dead, then why didn't Jordan say anything? On the other hand, this thing was smart. It might've snapped Jordan's neck and decided to play dead to draw them out. Neither option was desirable since both meant that Jordan was either injured or, well, worse, but they couldn't wait in silence forever.

Deon took a fearful step forward and immediately drew back. They heard a grunting sound from within the dark cave. It didn't sound inhuman, but at this point, it was sort of hard to tell. The firm lines between man and monster may be clear in the light, but under the cover of darkness, they become nearly indistinguishable.

The grunting got louder, bubbling into a primal yell. It was then that they could tell that it wasn't the creature

THE BEAST OF BEAR-TOOTH MOUNTAIN

at all. Unless this was some great deception, they were sure that it was Jordan who had come out the victor.

Minutes passed as they listened to Jordan's grunting, groaning, and heaving in the dark. After the battle, the flashlight was knocked in a way where the beam was pointed towards the tunnel. This kept Deon and the Reverend from watching whatever the young man was doing. They could only listen and hope that there was some decent explanation by the time he returned.

And he did return. Moments later, they heard the pitter-patter of Jordan's boots as the white beam drew nearer to them. Jordan and the light stopped at the edge of the tunnel and tossed something solid to the ground. Whatever it was, it made a large and wet thud upon hitting the floor. Putting the flashlight under his arm, Jordan cleaned the battled-hardened sword once again, which looked as if it had been bleeding itself.

"It's done," Jordan stated, a bit groggy in his speech. "Can I have some water?"

Deon immediately tossed his bottle to Jordan, who drank ferociously. The others soon joined him at the entrance and huddled around the object he had brought as a trophy, proof of their exploits.

It was the creature's head.

Its deformed and lifeless eyes stared out at them as its gaping jaws screamed in agony. One could hardly make out the pale color of its skin underneath the bloodstained flesh, which coincidently matched the reddish color of its hair.

Jordan shone the light down on the giant's decapitated head as the Reverend studied it carefully. He closed the creature's ungodly eyes and kicked it once for good measure.

It was true. It was dead.

"Leave that horrid thing behind," the Reverend said.

Jordan and Deon didn't argue. While any proof of such a monster was admittedly hard to come by, there was nothing the young men wanted more than to leave all this behind them. At this point, the story didn't matter anymore, only its outcome. They resolved to explain away any injuries or later complications through the lens of an unknown "beast" that came at them in the dark.

They were less likely to be institutionalized that way.

Jordan tossed the monster's head into oblivion. On the off chance that it might reattach itself, he aimed in the opposite direction from the corpse. After hearing a loud smash echo throughout the grotto, he was satisfied. The Reverend offered to refill Deon's bottle, and as soon as he returned the group set off once again. Having overcome the last of their trials, they were now free to enjoy their brisk walk back down the mountain.

They stopped only once near the entrance to reclaim the rest of Deon's belongings. Though they had no desire to ever lay eyes on the giant again, Jordan and Deon couldn't

THE BEAST OF BEAR-TOOTH MOUNTAIN

help but look over the pictographs one final time. Had they only heeded these ancient warnings, maybe none of this would have ever happened. But, if not them, then some other sorry souls might've been preyed upon by the beast, and it may never have lost its head.

After a final goodbye, they passed through the darkened film that covered the mouth once more and stepped out into something they hadn't expected. The night had faded, and the shadows were retreating as the sun was beginning to blossom over the remarkable horizon. The reds and pinks painted the morning sky as golden rays cut through the clouds. They couldn't make out the full picture through the trees, but it felt otherworldly. If only they had reached the summit, they might've been able to soak it all in.

"It has been a considerably difficult day," the minister began, gazing towards the east. "But, given that we are not so far from the top, it may be worth your while to do what you came here to do."

The boys looked at one another and thought about the preacher's words. They hadn't considered finishing the hike. Their fragile bodies could hardly stand, and as they held each other upright, they recognized that without the other, they wouldn't have made it this far.

And yet, something didn't sit right with them about leaving Bear-tooth Mountain without doing exactly what they had come here to do. Though they couldn't feel their toes, they resolved to reach the top.

"If we don't do it now…" Deon began.

"We never will," Jordan finished.

Before long, Jordan and Deon made it to the top. Though they waddled along like two marred penguins, they climbed as high as they could. They'd been much closer than either of them had realized, and had they not been so broken and bruised, they would've made it there in half the time. Given Scout's condition, the Reverend had opted not to follow but waited patiently behind. He needed the rest.

Finding refuge on a snow-covered slab, they plopped down and leaned back into the last boulder this high upward. They could see everything for miles. Every farm and ranch, every highway and byway, and every shadow that shrunk back from the light. Up here, they saw it all. The purple hues in the sky bled into the red as the sun highlighted every scarce cloud with a golden glow. If there were angels up there painting the sky, they were the best artists either of them had ever had the pleasure to see at work.

These two didn't know it, but from the top of Bear-tooth Mountain, they could see three, nearly four, different counties, and well past the state line. As the highest peak for over a hundred miles in every direction, Bear-tooth Mountain stood tall as a watchful guardian over these

THE BEAST OF BEAR-TOOTH MOUNTAIN

lands. No wonder the Natives thought it was sacred.

The young men sat there quietly, gazing at the new world around them. Between the heavens above them and the horrors below, they were completely overcome. They sat there together, weeping as they took it all in. Everything they had been through. Everything they had done. The fear, the rage, and the sorrow contrasted with the hope, the beauty, and the joy they felt. It all flooded through them like a river just after the snowmelt.

Of the two of them, Jordan cried the longest.

When he had finished, they clambered to their feet. Neither one of them said a word. Instead, they embraced. They held each other there for a long time while the warm sunlight bathed upon them.

They were forever changed men.

By the time Jordan and Deon had returned, the minister had changed Scout's bandages, cleaned her wounds, and prayed over her numerous times. Since she was in better spirits, they could only assume that Reverend Jude's liturgical petitions had done the trick. The Reverend himself looked rejuvenated after the extra bit of rest, and they soon started back on their way.

"The vet will be in by now," the Reverend added. "I would like to call her before the day gets away and she is needed elsewhere."

MICHAEL JOHN PETTY

Their descent was much quicker than the initial climb, thanks in part to the marker they had placed on the trail. Their boots sunk into the slushy snow as they trampled on down through the forest. They could hear the birds singing throughout the trees and caught glimpses of a few critters scurrying across their path. The mountain seemed alive in a way it hadn't been before. The creatures of the forest were no longer afraid, and they seemed to welcome their unscheduled visitors as they wandered triumphantly through the woods. They even spotted a herd of deer.

"The wildlife wasn't nearly as active yesterday," Jordan noted.

"I would think not," chuckled the preacher. "Animals can sense things that are far beyond our comprehension. Many of these likely avoided the mountain. Once the beast was slain, they had no reason not to flock back to their homes."

"You really think they knew about the giant?" Deon asked.

"Of course," the Reverend replied. "Many around these parts have heard the stories, though fewer believe them. Be it our supposed advancements or our insistence that myth and legend are nothing but, human beings try to explain everything away. Especially the true things that scare them. But the rest of creation cares not for fairy stories. They see things plainly as they are."

Time passed as they ambled on, and the minister soon

THE BEAST OF BEAR-TOOTH MOUNTAIN

left the young men behind. He insisted on getting Scout the proper medical treatment, and since Deon had gotten a bit slower, he wagered that he could get her to the animal clinic in enough time to still see them off. "Make yourselves at home in the church," he said. "I will return shortly to make us a fine meal before you go." With that, the minister turned away and carried on, as if the discussion had come to its natural end.

"He's insistent," Deon said.

"Pushy is more like," Jordan replied. "But he was right about all this."

"For all the good that did us…"

"I'd like to think that there's a world where we would've listened," Jordan said, fumbling around with the hilt of the Reverend's sword. "But honestly, I'm not sure anything would've convinced us. Or, convinced me at least."

Deon took a swig of his water bottle and let out a soft smile. "Me neither."

Jordan was comforted knowing that he wasn't the only fool on the mountain. But more than that, he was glad that his friend didn't see him as foolish.

"I should've told you about the move earlier," Deon said. "It seems so stupid after all of this, but I was afraid that you'd shut me out. I was worried that… Well… You'd think I was abandoning you."

"You were right," Jordan said. "You know me, I don't have many friends, and…" He noted how pathetic he was about to sound. "Before college, I didn't have anybody. Sure, my parents, but nobody I felt that I…"

"That you could relate to." Deon didn't know the feeling himself, but he'd seen it plenty of times on Jordan.

"I'm excited for you," Jordan continued. "I really am. You're gonna do great out there."

"Thanks, that means a lot."

Jordan nodded, this time genuinely. "I think I'm going to do it," he said abruptly, changing the subject.

"Do what?" Deon asked.

"Ask Chloe out. I really like her, and I think it's time."

Deon's eyes grew wide. "I think she likes you."

"Really?"

"Yeah, man! Why else would she always wait around and talk with you? There's something there, I'm telling you."

"I hope you're right," Jordan said. "Because I'm going for it."

"There he is!"

It wasn't much longer before Jordan and Deon made it back down the mountain. After passing through the parted sea of trees, they reached Jordan's Highlander and took another breather. Placing their packs in the trunk, they wandered over to the church building across the street, wishing they'd done so a day earlier. They hadn't noticed before,

THE BEAST OF BEAR-TOOTH MOUNTAIN

but a graveyard lay behind the church. Fresh flowers decorated nearly every gravestone, which looked pristine. Deon couldn't help but think of the Reverend's wife and wondered where on the premises she might be buried. But he didn't think about it long.

Jordan opened the thick wooden door and they entered without so much as a knock. After all, they'd been invited to waltz on.

The sanctuary wasn't much to write home about. Eight short rows of pews on either side of the aisle, a piano in the left-hand corner, and a pulpit up front with a large cross behind it. It was exactly how you'd picture an old country church stationed in the middle of nowhere. But what caught their eyes were the beautiful stained-glass windows that decorated the sides of the hall, each depicting a different Bible story in glittering detail. Those on the left-hand side were especially dazzling, but that was probably because of the morning light shining through. They turned to see another doorway to their right, this one wide opened and leading into a mess hall.

They could picture the Lord's Day morning brunches that might've taken place here following one of the Reverend's Sunday sermons. A dozen or two congregants dishing up, swapping stories, and leaving after a delightful fellowship. There may be some music playing, there may not. They could almost hear the minister saying grace over the meal before they all dove in.

MICHAEL JOHN PETTY

Within minutes, the Reverend entered through the back door of the kitchen area that led out to his parsonage just behind the churchyard and across from the cemetery. He had already handed Scout off to the vet and was carrying a first-aid kit with him. "Now, who would like to go first?"

Jordan offered Deon as tribute, and the minister began work on replacing his previous bandages and properly treating his wounds. The burns on his back, as uncomfortable as they were, were relatively mild compared to what they would have been if he'd been stripped naked. These would only take a few weeks to heal. It was those on Deon's neck and heels that concerned the Reverend most, and he treated them the best he could. He was a bit worried that the young man might also have a concussion, so he suggested the usual remedies and treatments. Mostly, that he shouldn't watch television and had to avoid anything mentally taxing. Once finished, the old man gave Deon some painkillers and moved to Jordan.

Thankfully, Jordan's wounds were less severe. Like Deon, he had quite a few cuts and bruises, but no burns that he could see or feel. The pain in his leg had returned after slaying the giant, though he didn't make a big fuss about it. Even after coming down from the mountain, he didn't want to take any attention away from Deon, who had it much, much worse. He'd thought of having the minister pray over it again but ultimately decided against it. To him,

THE BEAST OF BEAR-TOOTH MOUNTAIN

the jabbing ache would be a constant reminder of his battle with Death, and how it nearly took him. The minister was through with Jordan in half the time and jumped back to the kitchen to get a start on their victory feast.

"Where'd you learn all this anyway?" Deon asked.

"Before I was a minister, I briefly served my country as a medic overseas," the preacher began. "It was an honor to serve, but I hoped to do so by saving lives instead of taking them. Soon after, the Lord called me into ministry, beckoning me to aid Him in saving souls eternally. Not that *I* can save anyone, mind you…"

"Well, you certainly saved us," Jordan said.

"You did much of the work yourself," the Reverend replied. "Giant-slaying is not an old man's game, you know."

Jordan was embarassed when he remembered that he was still wearing the Reverend's sword. He went to unhitch the blade from his side when the elderly minister put a silent hand on top of his.

"It is yours," he spoke softly. "I have no more use for it. Let it be a marker of what happened here today, and how you may live tomorrow."

"Reverend, I can't take this," Jordan said in protest. "This is your birthright, your legacy. It's not mine to hold, let alone keep."

"It is now. That sword was meant for only one purpose. You have completed that purpose, and thus it rightfully belongs to you."

Unable to deny the minister's request, Jordan accepted the gift. With the Reverend's blessing, he named the blade *Giantsbane* in honor of the minister's descendants who had safeguarded the mountain for over a century.

Jordan and Deon didn't stay much longer. The Reverend had thrown together a quick meal consisting of buttermilk pancakes, some scrambled eggs from his coup out back, thick slices of bacon from a farmer down the way, and orange juice, freshly squeezed. No five-star restaurant could compare, and the young men were as satisfied as fattened lambs.

Over breakfast, the minister poked and prodded about their lives just as they had with his. By the time Deon got to his new job, the old preacher was elated.

"I know of a man in Provo you should get in touch with," the Reverend said as he slipped Deon a piece of paper with a name, phone number, and address written in perfect cursive. "He is a good man. A bit eccentric, but faithful."

That gave Jordan a chuckle.

"And what of you, giant slayer?" the Reverend asked Jordan, noticing he had yet to share. "What will you do next?"

Jordan thought long and hard about his answer, but in the end, he felt he didn't have much to offer. "I don't know," he finally said. He looked down at his sword and thought on their adventure. If he could face a man-eating

THE BEAST OF BEAR-TOOTH MOUNTAIN

giant and live, he didn't need to fear what the future might bring. "But right now, I think I'm okay with that."

The minister nodded in agreement. "The right path will come when it is time for you to walk it," he said. "Just be sure not to miss it when it does."

After breakfast, Jordan helped the minister clean up while Deon warmed the car. There weren't many dishes, and between the two of them, they made quick work of it. They made small talk about the weather, and the Reverend made Jordan promise to come and visit him again, even after Deon was gone. The young man agreed to make a yearly pilgrimage to Carmel, promising to come on a Sunday so he could see the preacher in his natural habitat.

"I'm in your debt," he finally said. "Thank you for saving me."

Reverend Jude placed a warm hand on the young man's shoulders and smiled. "You owe me no debt, but remember this, there is only One who has the power to give life and take it away. You are a knight now, honor your King."

Jordan and Deon had a hard time saying goodbye to the minister, though they were happy to be leaving the mountain. After some long embraces and many thanks, they climbed into Jordan's Highlander, made a slow U-turn around the Reverend, and stopped on the road facing east. Jordan traded quick but meaningful glances with the minister before placing his foot gently on the gas.

The Highlander picked up speed as it bustled down

MICHAEL JOHN PETTY

the country highway. Looking back in the rearview, Jordan saw that Reverend Jude still stood there watching them. After nearly a mile, the spiritual shepherd ambled back towards the churchyard and Jordan put his eyes back on the road.

"What time is it?" Deon asked, his eyes wandering out the window.

Jordan glanced down at his watch. To his surprise, it was broken. A large crack ran down the center and the arms had somehow gotten bent. *It must've happened in the caves*, he thought to himself before unbuckling it from his wrist and tossing it into the backseat. "It's early," he said.

"Wake me up when we're close to home," Deon said as he settled into the passenger's seat. "Those pancakes really did me in."

"As you wish," Jordan replied.

With a soft smile, Jordan raced on down the empty highway. Past the small town. Past the open fields. Past the gas stations and truck stops. Before they stumbled upon the cave, Jordan thought that he might dread the drive back, knowing that life as he knew it was about to end. He thought that the moment they got home would be it for them. He now realized how absurd that thought had been.

Jordan considered his future for a long time. He meditated on the Reverend's words, his pleas for Jordan to accept a higher calling. Yesterday, he would've disregarded all that as primitive superstition clung to by ignorance. But

124

today, he saw the world a bit differently. As he drove toward the horizon, he was thankful for the daylight as it illuminated the road before him.

As he watched the Highlander fade into the distance, Reverend Jude turned back towards the church. He hobbled his way over to the front door and felt a small chill creep over his shoulder. He felt as if a presence was lurking behind him; like he was being watched very closely. The minister turned to face the mountain once more, staring it deep in its eyeless face. Nothing.

The giant was dead, and that was enough.

He turned back to the church and hopped inside; a tad bit quicker than usual as to avoid being grabbed at the heels by some undead demon from beyond. As the door shut behind him, a cluster of clouds swarmed above Bear-tooth Mountain.

They soon darkened, and a sound like thunder rumbled across the land.

ABOUT THE AUTHOR

Michael John Petty is a writer, podcaster, and an award-winning filmmaker with a B.A. in Film & Photography from Montana State University. When he isn't writing, he enjoys long scenic drives, mountainous hikes, volunteering at his local church, and a good Western. *The Beast of Bear-tooth Mountain* is his first published work of fiction, but it certainly won't be his last. You can subscribe to his newsletter, *Further Up & Further In*, on Substack.

He currently resides in North Idaho with his wonderful wife and beautiful daughter.

Made in United States
Troutdale, OR
10/26/2023

14025169R00082